Women Longing to Fly

For Thomas, who keeps me happily grounded and finds every lost thing.

Women Longing to Fly

Stories by
Sara Kay Rupnik

Published by   MAYAPPLE PRESS
                   362 Chestnut Hill Rd.
                   Woodstock, NY 12498
                   www.mayapplepress.com

ISBN: 978-1-936419-50-0
Library of Congress Control Number: 2015901720

The author wishes to acknowledge the journals where these stories first appeared:
American Literary Review: Comfort at the Sacre Coeur; *Antietam Review:* An Act of
Mercy; *Bottom of the World:* Discrepancies of Love; *Chautauqua Literary Journal:* The
Wedding Crasher; *Driftwood:* The FNB House; *Lilies and Cannonballs Review:* A
Wednesday in June; *New Works Review:* Decoration Day; *River Poets Journal:* Vernal
Equinox; *The Rambler:* Fly.

Cover design by Judith Kerman, adapted from a photo by Seyed Mostafa Zamani.
Used under Creative Commons; license at https://creativecommons.org/licenses/
by/2.0/. Book design by Amee Schmidt with titles in Poor Richard and text in
Californian FB. Author photo by Christopher Cariano.

Contents

An Act of Mercy

I bought the gun right after Sam left. I'm frightened, I told the guy at the sporting goods store. I have trouble sleeping. I hear noises.

He made sympathetic sounds and pulled out small silver pistols from under the glass countertop. They looked like the cap guns my brother and I had when we were growing up, and I almost said no, I wanted a real gun, but he spoke about them seriously, as if I were an ordinary customer. I had to put my fist against my mouth to keep from smiling.

His speech ended, and I looked up. He was waiting for me to respond to whatever he had just said.

You choose, I told him. I don't want anything too big, too heavy, too complicated, or too expensive.

You'll keep this in the house?

I'm not sure, I said, thinking this could be a test question. Does it matter?

He shrugged. This .22 could fit in your pocket or purse, he said, but you'll need a permit to carry it on you. He picked up the daintiest of the toy weapons and presented it to me in his palm. Try it, he said, smiling.

I wasn't ready. I figured it would come in a box with instructions. I hadn't counted on such personal attention.

It's not loaded, he insisted, shaking his head.

I realize that, I told him, lifting the gun quickly from his hand. I curved my fingers around its coldness. I liked the surprising heaviness of it, the sleek feel of it.

We'll need to wait a couple days to run the state police check, he said, and you'll have to get a gun permit at the courthouse.

I'll keep it at home, I said. You don't check on that, do you?

He laughed as if maybe I could be sane after all.

I started to give him a credit card and hesitated, considering the anonymity of cash. In the back of my mind I could hear my friend Alice reminding me that once a plan is put into action, there was no sense in trying to alter its course. I handed him my MasterCard.

He needed my full name for the state police check. Am I missus, he wanted to know.

I nodded, and he asked for my spouse's name.

I lost my husband, I told him, my eyes on the tiled floor.

I'm sorry, he said. Have you been a widow long?

He left, I said, he didn't die.

I'm sorry, he repeated. I nodded again, but this time I looked up. His eyes were clear and honest. His face was tanned and pleasant. Before Sam, and even when things were good with Sam, I would have found this guy attractive. I might even have flirted with him a little. Now I knew I was way too wild for him. I looked into his open face and decided I would only shock him.

I didn't go back to the gun store right away. A lot of disorder had accumulated in the weeks since Sam had walked out, saying he had to find himself or to understand himself or to find someone else more understanding. I was not quite clear which it was, but just as I was certain he was gone, I was also certain he would come back, and I wanted to be ready. I dusted furniture and polished woodwork and shined windows and imagined the moment of Sam's return.

I am in the kitchen. He comes in the back door. He gives me that look that means he is too emotional to speak. He looks at the floor and brushes back sandy hair with long fingers. And I don't speak, don't make it too easy for him to slide back into my life.

Finally, he looks at me with the hoarse laugh only I know is embarrassment and says softly, "So, can I come home?"

"Yes." I smile. "Always."

As he moves toward me with his arms outstretched, I pull the gun from the drawer with the potholders. I hold it straight in front of me with both hands and aim somewhere toward his right side. Upper shoulder would be good, I think, but he is a tall man and I don't want to damage his face or his jugular. His leg would be easier to hit, but I love to watch him move, his long limbs fluid and easy. It is one part of him I do not want to change.

I spent a lot of time thinking about what part of Sam's body would serve as the best target. The actual shot was hard to visualize, but the expression on his face was not. Disbelief, anger, panic, and then remorse would lap across his features in steady waves before I calmly squeezed the smooth metal home.

I wondered what kind of mark the bullet would leave. Would it produce a geyser of blood or a small, black burn? Would he slump over or jerk backward? Would he cry aloud or pass right out?

When the guy from the sporting goods store called, I was tempted to ask him, but instead said I would be in soon. At the store, he was friendly, but intent on instructing me on the safety catch and ammunition. I tried to look attentive, but nothing he said was within my grasp.

I grew to love the gun. I took it with me everywhere I went. I liked its hard bounce against my hip when I carried it in the bottom of my purse. I liked its cold comfort when I slid my hand under Sam's vacated pillow. Mostly, I liked the reassurance I could go anywhere and not feel threatened.

As autumn deepened without any word from Sam, I unwillingly awoke earlier and earlier each day. My mind picked through my list of grievances against him while I waited for the dark to pale to another gray dawn. I altered and justified and added to that list until I thought it was perfect. Then I replayed the scenario in the kitchen: Sam in the doorway, the hand through his hair, the hoarse laugh, the quiet plea, the gun in my hand, the calm squeeze of my finger, and Sam's face as he asked my forgiveness.

My friend Alice called at least once a week to broadcast second-hand news bulletins on Sam. Where he'd been seen, what he'd been doing, who he'd been with. None of what she told me sounded much different from what I knew of Sam when he was here. She begged me to come help out during the early shift at the truck stop. "Just until that new girl gets over her foot surgery," she promised.

I told her I'd think about it, but I had no intention of leaving the house for any length of time. I had to be here when Sam came back.

I began to wear an old flannel-lined jacket Sam had overlooked in his rush from our life. One early morning, I put the gun in its cavernous pocket and started walking. It was still dark. Fog hung like a web, and fallen leaves clumped to my damp soles. The sounds of my footsteps and the neighborhood dogs and the trucks on the interstate were muted. I kept to the side streets and passed only three cars. Their headlights picked out the movement of the swirling mist but not me, striding toward the edge of town.

Just as I reached the cemetery at the intersection of Grove Road, the sun burned through in one great dazzle. It touched my shoulder and twisted me toward the crest of the hill where a school bus moved through an arc of scarlet and golden trees. Something about that solitary bus on a dirt road lined with light struck me as terribly lonesome, and I turned back with my hand stilling the movement of the gun against my thigh.

I took Alice up on her offer at the truck stop the next day. I knew I needed to be with people again. And, I told myself, I would only work hours when Sam would be at his job.

I was surprised to find my old uniform in the back of the closet. My first job out of high school had been at the diner in town. Sam stopped there every morning for breakfast because his first wife liked to sleep late. When Sam married me, I figured I'd never waitress again.

"Still fits," I said, twirling before Alice as she came over to greet me.

"You are awful thin." She shook her head, but then smiled. "I'm sure glad you're here. Let me take your jacket." She reached for it, and I remembered the gun.

"Just show me where to put it, Alice. I need to learn my way around."

I hung it from a hook in the little pantry just off the kitchen. I was arranging it so the heaviness in the pocket was not noticeable when May came looking for me.

May and her second husband had started Ernie's Truck Stop when the interstate first came through here twenty years ago, and after Ernie died, May expanded.

"I had a fella in here last week," she told me, "who thought he needed my undivided attention. It was slow so I sat down to talk for a spell, when

I felt his hand crawling up my leg. I smiled real nice, told him it was time to leave, and when he didn't move his hand, I leaned over and burned him with a cigarette."

"I didn't know you smoked, May," Alice said.

"It was his cigarette."

"Oh." Alice fluttered off with an order of eggs and home fries.

May gave me a stern look. "I don't expect any of us to have to put up with that sort of nonsense."

I nodded, mentally counting the steps it would take to get me from the dining room to the jacket pocket in the pantry.

The breakfast and lunch shift was too busy to think about nonsense. The customers were mostly men, but not all truckers. I laughed at their jokes, and after a week, became an expert at playing dumb to suggestive remarks. I started hanging Sam's jacket just inside the kitchen door where the coffee makers were stationed.

"Those are real nice melons, honey," one guy jeered as I jostled across the room with two orders of cantaloupe.

"Gee, do you think?" I stopped and looked concerned. "I thought maybe it was a little overripe when I cut it. Hope it tastes okay."

The place usually cleared out for a time around ten-thirty, and May and Alice and I would sit in the back booth for a coffee break. May talked about the numerous men in her life, Alice talked about her husband and kids, and I listened to both of them.

"I am one tired girl." May kicked off her shoes. "I went to that square dance at the grange last night."

"This a new man, May?"

"More old than new." She grinned. "He was a real lively fella for his age though."

"Jim and I haven't been to a dance in years. We chaperoned the prom last year. We didn't do any dancing."

"How about you, Lila? You a dancer?"

"Not even close."

"You know." Alice sat up straight against the red vinyl. "I should fix you up with my cousin. His wife left him last year. Gives him a hard time about seeing his son. It's a sad thing."

She caught my look.

"Lila, it's been how many months now?"

"I'll just get us a refill." May walked back toward the kitchen in her stocking feet.

"He'll be back," I told her. "He always returns eventually. If he thinks I'm seeing someone, it might slow everything down."

"I've heard he is seeing someone."

"Who?"

"Karen somebody, a little blonde thing."

"The cashier from K-Mart?"

"Could be."

"I heard he was seeing her before he left."

"So what's with this sense of loyalty? I don't believe anyone should be alone for too long. It warps them or something."

"Well, you needn't worry there. I've been warped for quite a while now."

Esther Steele called me at Ernie's just as I was shrugging into my jacket.

"I don't know whatever made me think you would be an easy person to find."

"How are you, Esther? How's the baby?"

"He walks, he talks, he climbs out of his crib."

We laughed, and then her voice changed. "Listen, Lila, I'm afraid this is a business call."

My mind went blank and then I remembered Esther had gone to work as a paralegal after the baby was born. "What's wrong?"

"You know Sam's been in to see us?"

"Oh?"

"The papers are ready for your signature."

"Papers?"

"To initiate the divorce proceedings. Can you stop someday after work?"

My mind stopped, my thoughts evaporated.

"Lila, you have talked to Sam?"

"No, I haven't talked to him. I haven't seen him. I haven't had a chance to—" I almost said "shoot him", but my words had stopped forming.

"I understand. Would it be better if we just sent them to your attorney?"

"I really don't think I'm prepared."

"You do have an attorney, Lila?"

"I have nothing," I told her. "I'll be right over, okay?"

"We'll be here."

I grabbed my car keys and went out the door, grateful that May and Alice were deep in conversation at the end of the dining room. I could not face the traffic on the main route past the mall, so I took the back road that follows the creek, cuts over Thompson Hill, and comes out near the hospital on the north side of town.

I couldn't concentrate. My mind clung to the scene in the kitchen and replayed it. Sam in the doorway with his soft look and hoarse laugh, then my hands around the gun and his expression of hurt, his quiet apology.

I passed a slow-moving jeep and started up Thompson Hill. The road narrowed at the crest where boulders jutted from their hillside settings. I started downward. My mind struggled to see his face, to hear his laugh, his words, and to feel the weight of the gun.

At the bottom of the incline, a pickup was stopped right where the road curves into the one lane bridge over Limestone Run. The driver's door stood open, blocking what little room remained on the road. I stomped on the brake pedal, frustrated at the unexpected delay. The truck cab was empty, but I saw a figure moving into the woods on the right.

I closed my eyes and dropped my head to the steering wheel, overwhelmed by too many emotions. Anger rose above the others and pushed me from the car. The truck was still running, but I had lost sight of the driver. I waded into the underbrush alongside the road and shouted toward the dense clump of leafless trees. "Hey, what's going on? I almost plowed into the back of your truck."

The shot was close. The echo bounced off the truck behind me. I halted in a patch of milkweed, the seedpods split and empty. My hand closed on the gun in my pocket as a man wearing a camouflage jacket and carrying a rifle crackled out of the woods.

I stood my ground, the gun warming from my hand, but I was suddenly weary. Weary of waiting, weary of the delays in my life. The hunter came closer, and I noticed the streaks of blood across his chest. My head began to swim.

His mouth was set in a line. "I hit a dog. He came up from the stream." The man turned to look over his shoulder, past the truck and my car.

"You shot him?" I caught on now. "You shot someone's dog?"

"He was in bad shape." His defensive tone changed as he turned back toward me. "Hey, lady, are you okay?" He put his hand on my elbow.

"I'm okay." I moved away, trying to focus on my car.

"You look washed out. I'm real sorry if I scared you."

He insisted on walking me to my car, shutting my door for me, and made a big production of following me into town. I had told him I was on the way to the hospital to visit my husband. I couldn't think of any other plausible story for my sudden weak spell, and in a way, it seemed like the truth. I waved in my rearview mirror when I turned into the hospital parking lot. He waved and kept going. I drove through the lot and came out on the upper side of Broad Street.

Esther took one look at me as I walked into the office and got up from behind her desk. "Lila, I'm sorry. I didn't know this would be so much of a shock. I thought you and Sam had talked this out."

"It's okay," I said.

"It's never easy." Her tone gave me no comfort. She glided to her desk and picked up a folder. "Do you want to sign them now?"

I held out my hand. "I'll take them with me." The folder felt too light to contain anything as substantial as a marriage. I gave her a steady look. "How is he?"

"I guess he got the electrical bid for that new middle school over toward Burton."

"He's happy?"

"He seems to be doing all right."

I fanned my face with the folder. "So, what's the hurry with the papers?"

Her eyes took in the floor, the door behind me, everything but my face. "I guess," she whispered, concerned for her disloyalty to office policy, "Karen is pregnant."

I continued to fan, but I closed my eyes against the shimmer of the room, the glare of the lights. When I could focus again, Esther was staring at my sleeve. "Is that blood on your jacket?"

I glanced down the outside of my arm to my elbow.

Esther reached into her desk drawer and pulled out a white plastic bottle. "I have just the thing to take that out."

I took off my jacket to examine the smear of blood. The weight of the gun pulled the right pocket toward the floor, and hit heavily against my shin.

"I don't want to bother you, Esther, really, I . . ."

"No bother, Lila. I'm happy to help you."

I gathered Sam's jacket into my arms. "I'm just not ready for help today, okay?"

"Sure." Her voice was soft. "Just take it with you. You can bring it back when you return the papers."

I clutched all of it—the papers, the spot remover, the jacket—to my chest and walked toward the elevators. I thought about the hunter in the woods. I imagined him leaping quickly from his truck and bending over the dying dog, then scooping the creature from the road and carrying it gently into the trees, thinking only of relieving its pain.

A Wednesday in June

Emma heard the sounds that other people only imagined. She heard Beethoven in winter squalls that blew down North Street and drummed at Mrs. Fritz's front door. She heard Joni Mitchell in rain pattering newly-leafed maples. In the night, she heard insomniacs pacing in all parts of the city, their footfalls so annoying that Emma wadded cotton in her ears to sleep. In the morning, her ears unstopped, Emma listened for the day. She could not name the exact day or month or year, but she clearly heard the passage of time. She had, when necessary, counted quarter hours by Mrs. Fritz's mantel clock, hours by chimes of the campus carillon, and weeks by the clamor of garbage trucks in the alley below her window. The cry of geese, frantic in their flight, or the harmony of spring peepers in City Park pond, or the grating gears of snow plows determined her attire for the day. As she dressed, she listened for the voices, high-pitched and tinny, that echoed through the heating ducts and told her where to go and what to do. Morning marked the peak of Emma's patience, the time when she was most willing to wait, to listen, to fully cooperate.

She had not always listened. Especially not to weather. The elements, she liked to think, had no effect on her. One time, wearing her thick gray coat with many sweaters underneath, she had fallen to the ground near the gazebo in the town square. The crash of voices, the painful bleat of the ambulance, even the less harsh voices of those who touched her, filled the circle of sky above her and badly frightened her. To avoid another fall, another episode of having people undress her while their firm voices talked about the stroke of the sun as a bad thing, Emma had begun to listen for what she should wear.

In this season marked by the clatter of bird song outside her window and the screech of bats in the wall behind her head, she chose a loose shirt that hummed with red and orange flowers, whispery polyester slacks, tennis shoes, and her prized scarf. Emma knew that without her scarf, her hair—as heavy and brown as expensive leather—would sing too loudly around her ears, and she would miss hearing the voices. She folded the square of gold lamé into a triangle, framed it around her wide, serious face, and tied the ends at the base of her skull. "Be still," she said to her hair, "and know that freedom will come at the close of day."

A new stillness gathered at the center of her little room, and Emma listened to the high, thin call that floated through the metal floor grate and vibrated the empty glasses on her card table. The time had come, it told Emma, to begin her journey.

She packed her paper shopping bag with sweaters and a handful of library books, *Merck's Manual* and *Fodor's Europe '96*, Martha Stewart magazines, Emilie Loring and Eugenia Price paperbacks, and crept as lightly as a cat down the outside staircase. At Mrs. Fritz's bedroom window, she paused to count the long breaths of sleep, to whisper silent assurances that another paid companion would come along to listen to Mrs. Fritz's USO stories and run her errands, but that she, Emma, must journey forth.

Another vibration sliced the sky, and Emma hurried on as the carillon rang six times. Few cars roared on the streets just now. She passed City Park and turned south at the Twenty-Sixth Street Library. The book return box clanged shut on books deposited by a man in a navy blue suit. He hurried past her to the car waiting in high idle at the curb. His hard black shoes were discordant. "Step softly," Emma proclaimed as she saluted his starched back. "Do not tread on the undisciplined ones who await your word."

Gravel from the library parking lot crunched under her rubber soles, and she stopped to salute its brick facade and announce the termination of her service. "I must not tarry here in the shadows of the grotesque. I must go forth into the world of the light and lively."

She would not miss the gray basement room where she had ruled, alert to pounce on the first deafening ring of the phones and carefully insert the numbered tapes requested by the voices. Once, on a slow evening, she had tried to listen to Tape 72, Childhood Immunizations, but she could not bear the disagreeable images it brought to her mind.

Emma wondered briefly if she would miss Mrs. Wyndham, the librarian in charge of the volunteers in the Tel-Med department. Mrs. Wyndham had encouraged her to stay on long after she had served her hours for the littering fine. "You have a wonderful speaking voice, Emma. We could really use you here." Mrs. Wyndham would have patted her shoulder, but Emma pulled away before the outstretched hand touched her, and the librarian nodded in understanding.

By the time Emma reached the western edge of the city, long, gangly children had appeared, clumped on the sidewalks with their basketballs slapping the pavement unceasingly, their laughter too large, and their shouts too hard on her face. Water swooshed from green hoses in rainbow arcs, tap-tapping as it fell at her feet. She marched, left, right, left, right, her feet and arms synchronized to the beat of the words she repeated from under her scarf. "Man will choose his destiny and follow it toward its end. He will not falter nor flinch in his pursuit of truth and honor."

Emma reached the highway, where the tumult of traffic in the northbound lane and the whine of mowing machine in the median bounced against her. She put out her thumb and her eyes followed the quick movement of the cars that sped by her. "Behold," she told them, "the day will come when you will rust and fade and die and I will live on, in spite of your judgment of me." At the end of her fifth recitation, a small blue car slowed and pulled off at the underpass. She strode toward it, holding a hand to her forehead to keep her scarf in place.

The little car held a young couple in high-backed bucket seats. They waved and she opened the back door and slid onto the ivory plush like the swish of a broom over dust. She crumpled her bag between her feet and nodded at the smiling man behind the steering wheel. "Airport, please," she told him, using the voice that requested little conversation and no questions.

Emma now noticed the plastic tub-like seat beside her contained a sleeping baby. Its head lolled to one side in its red cap, and bubbles formed at its mouth with each breath.

"Three months, tomorrow," the man was saying over his shoulder although Emma did not think she had spoken first. She nodded with her eyes still on the infant. It was the closest baby she had seen in years, and it was hard to focus on the car sounds and the people sounds with it so near. The woman was speaking to her now.

"I beg your pardon." Emma turned toward the voice with an effort.

"I asked if you had children," said the woman, her face cut by a smile.

"Yes." Emma tried to mirror her face in the woman's. "Three. But they're older. Not babies." These were lines she had practiced and could deliver with ease, but at the same time, she was certain she had had a baby once. She could never quite remember having it or losing it or even missing it, though she felt a sense of it with her at times.

Now the woman was asking for ages and a husband and a destination.

"Twenty-one," Emma said, "and nineteen and twelve. My husband's dead. My mother has the twelve-year-old. I travel."

The woman turned away, and Emma hoped it was from satisfaction with her answer, that she had chosen the correct responses. She knew her voice was just right, but the words came hard. She watched the baby sleep and wanted, in a sudden brief flash, to uncurl its tight fist with her finger. Surely her baby had been as perfect as this one, and the man with soft touches and the hard stabbing name, Jack or Ted or Mike, had only been an implement in her work of creation.

The woman turned to face Emma again, but there was no smile. "Where, exactly, did you say you were going?"

There was something important here, Emma knew. More important than the words that formed the question. Her lines were gone. She gathered her bag into her lap as if to check an itinerary. "Savannah," Emma said, reading from a paperback title.

"Georgia?" the woman asked.

"Certainly," Emma said in three beats. "I am expected in Savannah at six this evening. Family matters."

The baby whimpered to wakefulness, its eyes open and blue and clear. The mother cooed; the baby wailed, twisting in its seat and waving angry arms. Then it slid sideways, crumpling inward, and registered surprise at Emma. The cries stopped, the blue eyes smoothed.

"He likes you," the mother said. "Would you hand him to me? He needs to eat."

Emma considered the network of straps, the tiny arms, the malleable body, and looked out the window. "I have to get out here," she said.

"It's another half mile to the exit," said the man.

"It is," Emma told him, "my time to leave."

The man braked quickly, and the baby screamed. Emma gathered her bag to her chest and opened the car door. "Your child," she said, turning to salute the couple, "will grow and prosper among men. You will be rewarded with long life and many grandchildren."

She turned toward the off ramp. The thunder of planes broke the sky. The earth cried under her feet. The wind screamed as it tore at her scarf.

The swoosh of the opening doors eased the pain around her head, but the movement of people and luggage through the corridors jangled distractingly. Emma marched forward remembering that hesitation could precipitate loss. Left. Right. Left. Right. She was careful to square her turns, to keep her beat, and soon she found a large humped chair the color of grapes with a clear table in front of it for her bag. The man to her right gave her the look of the disturbed, so she pulled out a paperback to push his eyes away from her.

She waited, knowing all journeys took undetermined amounts of time.

When the sun changed patterns on the floor by the potted tree, Emma went to find food, leaving her bag on the chair to mark her place. She returned quickly, but not entirely satisfied with the choices she had made. The fizzle of her canned drink and the crackle of the bag with the soft candy were irritating.

A couple now sat in the grape chair across the table from her. The girl, long-legged and laughing in gasps that sounded painful, sat across the man's legs. He spoke directly into her ear so that she laughed again. They looked at Emma, and the girl put her bright head against his dark one. "There's one for you." She ran her fingers over his shirt buttons and watched Emma for a reaction.

The man's voice was low and rippling. "Let's go get a sandwich."

The girl raised up, twisting her back to him. "What's in your bag?" she said to Emma.

Emma put candy into her mouth and chewed carefully, hoping to stop the words of the girl.

"I said, what's in your bag? All your earthly possessions?"

Emma kept chewing.

The man pushed the girl from his legs and stood. "Come on, Kerry." He took her wrist.

The girl pulled at her slippery dress where it rubbed unhappily over her hips. Her black purse, large as a shopping bag, rattled against her leg. "Here, I'll give you a dollar just to let me see your bag. Whaddya say?" She held out a bill and smiled so hard Emma could hear her freckles scrape together.

The man moved away, towing the girl behind him. "Take your goddamned hands off me," she said, her words hanging in the air as they parted.

When Emma heard her summons, she began to walk earnestly, careful not to cause a commotion among those around her, watchful of the men with guns in their belts. The hallways became wider, the people fewer but more harried. The air around them rang with purpose, with a sense of mission. Ahead, she could see long rolling tables and men and women with shiny badges and sharp voices. Emma stopped, no longer certain of her mission. She put her hands to her scarf to silence the noise before her, but her eyes made out the words of the couple, who now stood along the windows, lost in their anger.

"You never wanted me to go with you at all, did you?" The Kerry-girl cried. Her hands clenched at her sides. Her purse dragged on the spotted carpet. The glass at their backs shook.

"Of course, I want you with me." His voice pleaded; his face darkened. "We've planned this for how long now?"

"Then how dare you lecture me like some dull child?" The arm holding the dark strap of her purse rotated as perfectly as the blade of a windmill, and sent the black leather walloping against his shoulder with the sound of breakage.

His hands came to the girl's shoulders, squeezing until she flung her head back. He talked to her face in the hoarse whispers of unformed welts.

"I thought you were so special." The girl shook off his hands. "I'm strictly for show, and that's it. For display purposes. You bastard, go by yourself."

The girl turned, her long legs charging away from the man who leaned against the window, his head bent.

Even with her ears covered, Emma thought the departure of the girl seemed too loud to bear. The sad anger hung in the emptying corridor as Emma watched the girl turn from sight, the purse and her uneven laughter swinging behind her. Emma marched in the direction the girl had taken, sidestepping a last flurry of people forging toward her with red and yellow promises held in their hands.

There, just ahead, the Kerry-girl stood by a pillar in the center of the concourse. She was a continuous movement of black against white as she emptied her purse into the cage-like basket at her feet. Squares of color, squares with faces, squares with writing sifted downward, followed by the clash of keys and a silver chain. When the girl strode away, Emma heard the hum of her own destination. And when Emma reached into the basket to touch the red and yellow folder, every part of her body sang together like a great cathedral choir.

Emma retraced her steps into the quieter corridor. She concentrated on making her steps steady and firm, no longer marching, but not skating like a dancer's. She heard the sigh of the red and yellow paper in her hand and looked down. The letters did not form words, but images of the sea and mountains and clear air chimed like a halo of bells under her scarf.

A woman in a shiny badge shouted at her. "Ticket and identification, please."

Her mind stuck on the meaning of identification, Emma handed over the red and yellow folder. When the woman opened it, a card bearing the Kerry-girl's face fell to the floor. Hurriedly, the woman bent to retrieve it, her eyes on the thin strip of oaktag. "You should have been at your gate an hour ago," she told Emma. "Your plane is due to depart."

Emma glided toward the rolling table, her destination in her hand. Mercifully, no disagreeable bells sounded. No one stopped her passage. As Emma waited for her bag to emerge from the silver box with a tattered curtain, she remembered the Kerry-girl's words. "I will take these, my earthly possessions," Emma said soundlessly. "I will move on, as it has been decreed, and not bend to the will of the cruel and unjust. I have been blessed by one who suffered for her cause."

At the gate to her destination, a jolly man took Emma's ticket and glanced at Kerry's photo without really seeing her pale face, her silver hoop earrings, her bright hair dyed black. "They're having a cold snap in Vancouver right now," the man boomed at Emma.

Emma smiled politely and adjusted her scarf. "I have friends," she recited. "Friendship is the warmth of the soul." She picked up her bag and raised her hand to salute, but stopped mid-gesture and waved, a stiff, sideways motion that dismissed the shiny badges from her life.

Comfort at the Sacre Coeur

A tattoo was the perfect solution. Maura thought of it while painting her toenails in the backyard. She ran her fingertip, also painted in Melon Mist, across the small island of flesh between the bump of her ankle and the bone of her heel. Yep. Four numbers, small but legible, would be fine right there on the inside of her foot.

She peeled her sticky back away from the plastic webbing of the chaise lounge and stood up, pulling the straps of her three-year-old maillot back onto her shoulders. She was a tall, long-limbed woman, and she tried to imagine the tattoo, to consider its visibility when viewed over the distance from her head to her foot. She squinted at the chosen site, slightly above the level of the grass, and decided it would work nicely. It would be covered by the strap of her sandal in summer. In winter, it would look like a bit of lint caught inside her stocking. Even in her bare feet, Robert would never notice.

Maura was growing a little weary of her husband's obsession with her memory. "I'm worried about you," he'd say, giving her one of his clear blue stares as if he hoped to evoke a confession. "Maybe you should see a neurologist." She knew he was sincere, that he cared, but she could feel his concern turning to impatience.

She had carried the number with her for a while, wrapped around her ATM card on pink note paper. Robert found it while looking through her wallet for the owner's card to the Taurus. "Not a good idea, Maura," he'd said, shaking his heavy head, now silver at the temples, his face sad.

She wanted to tell him she had a good memory. She could remember birth dates for his entire side of the family, even the babies', which kept increasing in number. She could remember exactly what shelf in their branch library held the Robert Ludlum novels. She could remember song lyrics and the Apostle's Creed and most of the names of Santa's reindeer.

She wanted to tell him she knew this number once, too. She even knew these four digits were called PIN by the bank and she knew what words PIN stood for. But what, Maura wanted to ask him, did it matter? Really—in the scheme of life, as he would say—how significant could it be?

She had copied the number in the back of her address book, and then she wrote it on the flat of her palm whenever she went shopping. The ink smeared against the steering wheel. The cashier looked at her with narrowed eyes when she opened her hand for change. She had trouble washing the ink from her skin.

With this new solution in mind, Maura remembered her friend Holly once had a biker boyfriend with tattoos. She waited, as she often did, for Holly to make her morning run past the house and flagged her down with a glass of orange juice.

Holly couldn't place him. "Are you sure it was me, Maura?" She spoke in quick breathy gasps.

"Yes. He was short with dark hair. Had a one-syllable name. Bill or Bob or Brad. Something like that."

"And where, exactly, was his tattoo?" Holly asked. She ran her small hands through the ends of her sun-bleached hair and frowned as if she were anxious to get on with her run or as if she too was worried about Maura's memory.

"Right shoulder." Maura could see the delicate dragonfly clearly, resting beside his black tank top, at the top of his narrow back. Every slender vein in its wings shone with color. "Boyd," she told Holly. "His name was Boyd."

"Boyd Latimer," Holly said at once, starting to smile. "I haven't thought of that man in years. Why would you remember his tattoo?"

"I liked it." Maura thought about how, in a certain light, the dragonfly looked as if it were resting on Boyd's shoulder, wings quivering, ready at any moment to take flight.

Holly, appearing freshly tanned in her electric blue spandex, took Maura to a more recent boyfriend named Lance. Lance worked for the state agricultural lab, collecting data on migratory birds. He wore his red hair cut at an angle across one eye like one of the skateboarding kids in Maura's neighborhood. He was glib, not the least bit interested in why Maura would want four numbers on her ankle.

"Sure thing, sweetie. Have a seat." He jumped up from his desk chair and indicated she should take his place. "We band the birds for identification, but I've done animals before," he told her while readying his equipment. "For lab experiments at school."

He propped her slender foot on the pull-out writing surface of his desk, cushioned her heel with a scratchy white towel, and went to work with his electric stylus. Maura didn't watch. She concentrated on the gentle pressure of his freckled hand, as he held her instep and adjusted the position of her foot from time to time. She kept her eyes averted to an ancient painting, the oil colors crazed and crumbling, of a clipper ship. She was grateful for Holly talking the entire time of other things, birds and weather and people she and Lance both knew. Nothing that required Maura to respond.

"That's it, babe." Lance tugged on Maura's toes and she looked down at his work. She bent her knee and pulled her foot across her lap to study it closer. The numbers were small but, she decided, they would be easily readable once the swelling went down.

"It's fine," Maura said. She took the hand he offered to help her stand. She shook out the bunches in her cotton print skirt and slid her feet back into their leather thongs. "What do I owe you?"

The tattoo served its purpose. Maura went shopping without panic. She pushed the buttons on the ATM machine with confidence, one eye on the red mound of her ankle.

"I think that mosquito bite on your foot is infected," Robert told her one night as they sat on the porch. He had been reading the paper. She had been pulling dead leaves from her geraniums and impatiens. Now they sat facing one another, legs stretched out in the space between their chairs. "Let me look at it." He watched her over the top of his reading glasses, waiting.

She rose and carefully removed his glasses, slowly folding them and setting them on the table with the flower pots. She placed a hand on each arm of his chair and bent to kiss his forehead, his eyebrows, his eyelids. "You worry about me too much." Her lips traced his left cheek, the crooked bridge of his nose, his right cheek. "You know that?" His warm mouth, the rough line of his jaw, his sweet neck.

He pulled her onto his lap and held her chin in his hand. "Yes," he said, "I worry." His fingers moved across her cheek. "I don't think it's too much." He held her so close she couldn't see his face. "I don't even know if it's enough."

Maura went to the emergency room the next day. She hated hospitals. Even the smell of alcohol made her queasy. She knew she had no choice. Her foot was no better, and going to her family doctor would be like going to Robert. They would both want to talk about why she had gotten the tattoo instead of simply treating the infection.

She wasn't sure where to park, but found a spot at the far end of the furthest lot, way past the circle on the pavement where Life Flight could land. She was careful about skirting the patches of tar that pooled in the sun-warmed asphalt. Her shadow looked extra long and gangly, her sleeveless dress too large for her narrow frame. Even her head seemed out of proportion to her body. She touched the ends of her loose brown curls, trying to remember when she last had her hair done. The automatic doors at the emergency entrance slid open quickly, as if someone were inside watching for her. She walked in, happy, at least, that she could walk.

The woman at the window of the emergency room office called her by name, as if she knew her. "How are you, Maura? Nothing serious, I hope." She had dark hair cut in a wedge and braces that caught the light when she spoke, but the only thing Maura could find familiar about this woman was the scent of Shalimar.

"No, not at all serious." Maura smiled at the woman in reassurance while noticing that her name badge said Carol Tilley. She took the information sheet from Carol's hand.

"I know we've got you on file." Carol started typing, her eyes on the computer screen. "It makes it easier for the doctor if you list your symptoms on that form."

Maura could think of little to say in the long white spaces that followed each question. She wrote "red, swollen left ankle. Possible infected insect bite."

When she took the paper back to the window, Carol told her how good she looked. "Dr. Compton's on duty this morning. He'll be happy to see you."

"Great." Maura nodded although she couldn't imagine why a strange doctor would be that excited over a one-time patient. She moved to the part of the waiting room furthest away from the window. The television was in this area, and the few other people waiting seemed absorbed in a game show.

They were called slowly, every half hour or so, by a nurse in a yellow pinafore. Maura tried to read an old *Ladies Home Journal*. She checked her ankle for sudden improvement or for a red line running up her leg. When she was alone, two women came in carrying two of the three small children they had with them. They settled on the orange vinyl sofa opposite the television. Maura watched them over the pages of the article on "Mid-Life Makeovers."

The mother tried to interest the baby in a television show where a man in a Navy uniform was trying to guess the price of a box of Creamettes. The boy started looking in his grandmother's purse for gum.

"I already gave you some gum," the mother said, slapping his hand away.

The little girl cried, twisting her head suddenly away. The grandmother patted her back. "Stomach flu," she said to Maura. "They've all had it."

The mother rolled her eyes at the grandmother. "I wish my Ex would get down here with his insurance card," She pointed to the little girl. "Her father," she said to Maura.

The nurse in the yellow pinafore came for Maura. At the doorway they stepped aside for a fast moving man in coveralls. Maura figured this had to be the father, anxious for word of his daughter. She was about to tell the nurse to take the whole crew—the little girl, the worried father, the irritable mother—take them all ahead of her. But the nurse had moved on and when Maura looked back, the mother and father were arguing. The toddler was crawling toward the magazine table, the boy was playing with the television, and the little girl lay on the couch while the grandmother stood to join the argument.

Dr. Compton didn't say much about the tattoo, didn't act like it was the sign of an unstable woman, but he did seem happy to see her. "How are you and Robert getting along? It's been what—a year now?" He spun around on the metal stool, leaned his dark head against the wall, and folded his long arms casually.

"Has it really?" she asked brightly. She tried to find a frame of reference, tried to remember why they should be so friendly with one another. "We're fine," she said. "It's been a quiet summer."

"You still go up to the lake?" He pulled his prescription pad from the pocket of his lab coat.

The lake. Maura tried to place this man, this face, among the people they used to see at the lake. "We didn't make it up there this summer. You know how fast summers go."

He looked at her a bit longer than she thought was necessary before he started to write. The circular loops on his letters looked familiar.

"This should work," he said as he wrote. "If it doesn't, come back." He handed her the prescription. "Tell Robert I asked about him."

"Yes, I will." She shook his hand. "Thanks."

She went to the hospital pharmacy because her local druggist always asked too many questions. Nothing too personal, just too friendly. "Now what did you do to your foot, Maura?" he'd say.

The pharmacy, the snack shop, the gift shop, and the chapel were located in the center hall opposite the hospital's main entrance. Like a hotel, Maura thought as she approached the cashier posted at the end of the hall nearest the lobby. The woman operating the cash register wore the pink smock of a volunteer and also seemed happy to see Maura.

"You look great," the woman told her, as if she had at one time looked bad or been in some way connected to this palace of illness.

"Well, thank you." Maura exaggerated her response, beginning to find this whole place a joke where the punchline was trying to see who could outdo the other in outrageous compliments.

"We were just talking about you the other day," the woman said now, pushing buttons on the cash register so the rings on her hand glittered with each movement. "How we've missed you coming around to talk to the other parents."

"Yes, well, I have always been somewhat of a talker, haven't I?" Maura took her package, a tube of antibiotic cream "to be applied twice a day to the infected area." She smiled, waited for her change with her ink-free palm, and tried to count the exact number of minutes before she could be out, freed from this bizarre case of mistaken identity. Less than five, she decided.

"There's a fella here now who could use you." The woman turned her platinum head to look towards the chapel door. Her earrings, a chain of three bronze coins in each ear, jingled slightly as she moved. "He was just here. His son is in Five West. He's alone. Maybe if you..."

"Monica," Maura said, reading the woman's name badge, "sometimes talk is cheap, you know?" She looked directly into the woman's clear green eyes under the perfectly groomed eyebrows and the pale jade eye shadow. "Sometimes absolutely nothing helps."

She walked away quickly, not toward the entrance, but down the hall hoping to find the emergency entrance again, hoping for a fast escape. She passed the chapel's heavy solid door, its gleaming wooden panels reflecting the white movement of her dress. She passed the glass front of the snack shop where people propped their elbows on the counter, holding their heads over cups of coffee, bowls of soup, a doughnut, a fried sandwich. She passed the windows of the gift shop where people wandered aimlessly, pausing to touch items as if they hoped to divine some great truth.

She recognized him at once. His youthful face was lined and unshaven. His once cheerful shirt was now limp and too large. He stood near the window, beside the small assortment of overpriced, cheap toys. He glanced up, meeting her eyes through the glass, and Maura thought she could be looking into a mirror. She walked through the door, into the shop, over to the toys. She picked up a pair of glasses that put rainbows around everything viewed through its lenses. She tried them on.

"Does that really help?" His voice was gravelly from too little sleep or too many cigarettes or maybe both.

Maura turned to look at him. A halo of red, orange and yellow covered his soft brown hair. "Do you want to talk?" She watched the shades of purple across his mouth for an answer.

She took him to the Sacre Coeur Motel on the edge of town. She couldn't remember stopping there before, but she remembered someone telling her it was built on the site of a Catholic church destroyed by fire in the early 1920s. She always imagined that it resembled a French monastery with its palest pink stucco and arched doorways. The name, encased in a pink neon heart, gave her comfort, as if she could expect a miracle here.

The room was disappointingly ordinary. It was decorated in blues and greens with a flowery bedspread and seascapes on walls the same pale green as ocean foam. There was no shrine, no altar, not even a branch of candles.

Maura stretched across the foot of the bed, her arms extended over her head toward the bathroom. Her feet hung over the side closest the door. She looked up at the ceiling, also pale green, with plaster swirled into craters and ridges. The lighting fixture had six legs and looked to

Maura as if it could be a land rover or whatever NASA called it, left behind by the astronauts on the surface of the moon.

The man remained standing near the door. His shoulders were hunched inside his shirt of bright palm trees. The short sleeves hung to his elbows. He had one arm braced against the back of the desk chair as if he might otherwise fall.

Maura patted the bed beside her. "It's water. Come float awhile."

He looked at his watch. He shifted his weight away from the chair to brush his other hand through his hair.

"How long do you have?" Maura asked, lifting her head to see him clearly.

"They said he'd be awake in a couple hours."

Maura watched the tug of the bed and the tug of the hospital play across his face. "I'll have you back in two hours," she promised, patting the bed again.

He walked unevenly, listing toward the bed, and then falling crosswise beside Maura, face down. He pillowed his head on his arms. "I feel like I'm stuck to these clothes," he said, and his voice was slow and deep as if drifting toward sleep. "I can't even remember how long I've had them on."

"Do you want a shower?"

"I want to sleep." His eyes closed and then re-opened wide and panicky. "I can't sleep." He sat up, his voice loud and cracked. "How can I sleep? I shouldn't be here." He bent his head into his open hands, his elbows on his knees.

Maura watched him, not moving, not reacting until he looked at her and wanted her to speak. "In two hours, when you go back, nothing will have changed. It will be exactly the same, as if you never left."

Maura could see he believed her, that this was what he wanted to hear. She did not tell him that the thing he most desired, this lack of change, would become the hardest to bear and, after days and days of sameness, he would welcome any change. She knew it was not something that could be told, and he would learn it soon enough.

He fell back onto the bed, which undulated under his body. He closed his eyes and sighed, arms at his sides. He pushed his toes against the heels of his scarred Nikes, sending them to the floor in soft thuds.

Maura held his hand and watched him sleep. She tried to imagine him without the lines in his face, without the stubble of beard and the hollows under his eyes. When he stirred, she rubbed his chest gently, like a mother soothing a child, and slowly unbuttoned his shirt. The blue buttons were as tiny as those on a baby's sweater. He opened his eyes and watched her face, but he did not move.

His ribcage rose from his thin frame like frail wings. She knelt beside him, her knees even with his jeans pocket. She placed her thumbs at the center of his chest and spread her long fingers along the crevices between his ribs. She moved her thumbs and the heels of her hands slowly, deftly, outward. "It's so nice to be touched." His voice was hoarse.

Her hands moved upward and the Desert Sand shade of her nail polish made a bright motion though his fine chest hair. "I used to give massages at the Y," she told him, surprised at herself for remembering. "A long time ago. In my younger days."

Her thumbs rotated under his collar bone and moved on to his shoulders. He turned onto his stomach as she eased his shirt away from his arms and tossed it toward the headboard. It smelled of sweat and cigarettes and something sweet, like bubblegum. She moved her hands over his back in long rolling movements before concentrating on the tightness in his neck and shoulders. His eyes were closed, but his voice was stronger.

"How long has it been?"

She could see the face of his watch from where his hand rested by her knees. "We have forty more minutes. No worry," she said without pausing in her movement.

"I mean since you lost your son."

Her fingers stopped circling, and she pressed her knuckles against the knotted muscle on his right side. "You need to relax, not talk," Maura said firmly.

He grasped her hand in his and twisted his body suddenly, catching Maura off guard. He pulled her down beside him so they were face to face, eye to eye. He squeezed her wrist, forcing her hand open. "Talk to me."

Maura had heard those words spoken in that tone before. She closed her eyes and saw Robert, his eyes the color of a flame's center and his face twisted as he shouted at her. "Please, Maura. Goddammit, talk to me."

She opened her eyes into the fierce brown stare of the man beside her. His naked chest looked pale and vulnerable. He was, Maura could plainly see, frightened. Frightened by the strangeness of a day that had started in a festive shirt, passed through the foreign horror of hospital corridors, and landed him in a motel room with a woman who had seemed, for however briefly, like someone he knew. Maura breathed in his scent, strong and acrid and sweet. She looked into his eyes as far as she could see, wanting to know as much as he did.

He pulled her to him and held her there as tightly as she could stand it. She kissed the salty skin at the top of his shoulder and closed her eyes, trying to will Robert into the place of this man. She imagined his firm full body, his smooth chest, his quick, hard hugs and warm mouth. The pale eyes that told her what she no longer asked.

When the man moved his arm, Maura knew he was checking his watch. "I need to get back." He kissed her forehead and rolled away from her.

"I need to make a brief phone call," Maura told him as he grabbed his crumpled shirt and headed for the bathroom. He nodded and Maura smiled at his quick, decisive movements. She stood, stretched her hands over her head, and walked to the desk where the pale pink phone sat with a heart painted in the center of its dial. She picked up the receiver, ready to call Robert as soon as the numbers came into her head.

The FNB House

There are folks who claim to know the exact moment their lives took on new significance. They might be climbing a mountain or grilling steaks or trying on bras at Victoria's Secret, and some obvious thing like a loose rock or a burst of flame or a triangle of lace will make them suddenly comprehend that they had been adopted or abused or fed too much sugar as an infant. Nothing that immediate has occurred with us Dunegans. Comprehension of our family life has come in pieces as tiny as those plastic bulbs from the Lite Brite we had when we were little. Plug enough colored pegs into backlit black paper, we figure, and we're bound to have something worth seeing.

Before she got religious and gave birth to Luke and Mary Ruth, Mama expected the rest of us to have those good Yankee things she had in her Pennsylvania childhood, things like a tall, strong house with a basement to protect us from tornadoes, and a big yard with thick green grass; never mind that basements and thick green grass didn't exist in Brunswick, Georgia. Better yet, Mama wanted us to live like a television family. Not "The Brady Bunch," which involved remarriage and two bunches of children, but an old-fashioned television family like Mama watched when she was a girl. "Father Knows Best" was her favorite.

"We Dunegans could be just like the Andersons," she said to Daddy on those good days when he was working steady and the rent was paid.

"We have our own Betty and Bud and Kitten." She gave Adrian, Christina, and me a wink. "Now if we only had a house like the Andersons. Something big and white with shutters and a porch."

"We have a porch, Mama." Adrian was always a bit of a know-it-all.

"Our own porch, honey. Not one we share with the neighbors."

Actually we didn't share the porch. It was neatly divided from the Quigleys by a floor to ceiling wall. And between ourselves, Christina and I decided we were more like the Brady Bunch than Mama wanted to admit. We knew Daddy had been married before, and sometimes, after a few beers loosened his tongue, he made odd claims. "My boys," he said sadly, "were good boys. I know that much."

"Now, Foster," Mama would respond, "we all know that Adrian is just the best boy there ever was." Since Adrian was hands-down Mama's favorite, we were positive Daddy's talk of *boys* somehow pertained to the brother in our midst.

In her search for our Father Knows Best house, which Christina called The FNB House due to her lack of spelling skills, Mama found herself a realtor with apparently nothing better to do than spend his summer driving Mama and her three kids around Glynn County. Not the tanned, outdoors type Mama usually loved to talk to, Edmund Window was the slight, wiry type with gray hair and a narrow moustache to match. He wore a nautical cap and drove a Cadillac the color of Mama's favorite fingernail polish. We thought of him as Captain Ed.

"Isn't this just the perfect day to look for our house, Ed?" Mama said every time he pulled up to our duplex on Richmond Street.

"Certainly is, Adele." He tapped his hat brim in a little salute.

Adrian and I loved that Cadillac for its smooth leather backseat, roomy enough for each of us to have our own circle of space. Christina loved the individual reading lights and the little ashtrays filled with matchbooks the same red as the car and lettered in gold. She slid a handful into her pockets every time we went out.

Captain Ed must have known we had no money for a house, especially not one of the big, historic houses on Union Street, which Mama said was the only decent street in all of Brunswick, but he treated us like serious buyers. We dressed the part, with Mama wearing one of her summer dresses and her good pair of sandals and Adrian, Christina, and me wearing shorts outfits bought especially for the Baptist Summer Vacation Bible School.

32

In the beginning, Captain Ed took us to several small ranch houses along the streets off Altama Avenue. "This is a maintenance-free house, Adele." He pointed out aluminum siding on soffit and fascia, while Adrian tore into the backyard and Christina and I fidgeted, waiting for him to unlock the front door and let us roam free. We were fascinated by how other people lived. We thrived on fingering their satiny bedspreads and thick, flowered towels, their polyester dresses and silk ties. We got a rush from peeking into their underwear drawers and petting the stuffed animals piled on their children's ruffled pillows. While Mama sashayed around the kitchen oohing and aahing over built-in appliances, Christina tried on rings from the little girl's jewelry box and I sprayed the mother's perfume under my t-shirt.

Later, when we were back in the Cadillac with Adrian covered in dirt or bug bites or grass stains and Christina pink-cheeked with guilt and myself reeking of Shalimar or Chanel No. 5, Mama gently broke the news to Captain Ed. "Not quite what we want, I'm afraid. A bit too small. Not enough yard."

"Not FNB," Christina mouthed in my direction.

Nothing seemed to deter Captain Ed. Every couple of weeks or so, he showed up at our house and we'd all pile back into the wine-red Cadillac for another day of househunting.

"Captain Ed likes Mama's stories," Christina said.

"Captain Ed likes Mama," Adrian boasted, as if Mama was a trading card only he possessed.

"Every man likes Mama," I said.

And she could tell stories.

"You may not realize this, Ed, but I'm not originally from the south." Mama's voice had never sounded less like a Yankee's.

"You don't say?" Captain Ed's voice was the drone of a horse fly.

Adrian yawned and curled into his leather corner, but Christina and I stayed alert, hoping to hear some new tidbit about Mama's Yankee childhood or Daddy's other wife. When Mama was caught up in her storytelling, she sometimes forgot we were present.

"No, sir, I grew up in a little tourist town in Western Pennsylvania. The only thing we had there was a big ole lake where the ducks walked on the fishes' backs."

"Are you pulling my leg?" Captain Ed's laugh crackled through the car like an electrical current, but Adrian slept on.

"Why of course you know I'm not." Mama's laugh was high and ringing. "No one could make up something that crazy, now could she?"

Our Mama had been fifteen years old and bored. She hated living in the same small town where she had lived all her life, and she hated her job at the frozen custard stand. She was sick of scooping custard into cones and blending milkshakes and making banana splits, but her only other job option was selling stale bread to tourists who wanted to feed the fish that the ducks walked over. "It was the epitome of boring!"

Faced with such dismal choices, Mama talked her best friends Zoe and Mary Ann into hitchhiking to California. "We can sleep on the beach," Mama told her friends. "We can find jobs. There will be music and dancing and boys who love us. It will be wild."

Mama could have sold snow to an Eskimo.

The girls changed into bell-bottoms in the Texaco restroom. They tied scarves in their long hair and dumped their schoolbooks in trash bins. They stood along Route 6, right there on the edge of Linesville, Pennsylvania, with their thumbs in the air and their gypsy earrings reflecting the sun. They were certain it would only be seconds before someone would drive along and send them home, so it was purely a miracle that the very first vehicle to happen along was a magnificent eighteen wheeler.

Since it's impossible to stop an eighteen wheeler on a dime, the girls had to run a ways to catch up. They looked up to see that the driver wore sunglasses and a wide, cocksure smile. He was the handsomest man in the world. "You ladies need a lift?" His drawl was like Elvis Presley's. "Hop on board."

He swung his sinewy self down from the cab with the ease of a cowboy and hoisted those fresh, young girls upward. As they slid under the steering wheel, they felt the throb of the engine vibrate into their bones, but not one of them had second thoughts. Zoe and Mary Ann took the narrow bench seat behind the man who was to be our Daddy, and Mama sat by his side.

"What's your destination?" Daddy asked as they roared off towards the Ohio line.

"California."

"That's a shame," Daddy said. "I reckon I can only take you as far as Cleveland. What will you all do in California?"

"Sleep on the beach."

"Dance by the ocean."

"Become children of love and peace."

The more they talked, the more Daddy realized his truck was no place for runaway girls. He, after all, was a man of honor, so all the way towards Cleveland he tried to discourage them. California was a long way to drive, let alone hitchhike, he told them. Surely nothing good could come from setting off on a journey with no more than their youth and beauty to sustain them.

Mama was entranced by this good-looking man who talked like a poet. The other girls rolled their eyes behind his back and asked him for cigarettes.

Daddy pulled over at a truck stop near Chardon. "I'll be happy to take you all back," he told them, "but if you insist on going farther, this here is the safest place to catch another ride."

"Open the door, Adele," Zoe said to Mama.

Mama pushed open the door, and they jumped to the pavement like paratroopers. Mama sensed Daddy watching her. He had taken off his sunglasses, and Mama saw the bluest eyes in all her life. "Adele," Daddy said, "I'd like to take you home."

"And that's exactly what he did, Ed," Mama said to finish her story. "He took me home and met my mother and before you knew it, we were married and living right here in Brunswick, Georgia."

"Like the end of a movie." Captain Ed's Cadillac glided up our street without a sound. We would have to shake Adrian awake, and then he'd be cranky. I sighed, and Christina turned to me, her eyebrows rising into her crooked bangs. No, we had learned nothing new today. In other re-tellings of this story, we had heard how Mama's girlfriends were fetched home by the cops or how Daddy's truck soared down Route 6 like a jet on takeoff or how the sun fell lower in the sky and made their faces glow red, but always the end was too quick and easy, too incomplete. Christina thought there should be more kissing and hugging in Mama's story, and I thought there should be more action. Like Daddy standing up to Grandma or fighting with another boy to take Mama away.

"We'll have better luck next time," Mama always said as Captain Ed drove off in his fine car.

The next time Captain Ed took to us a cottage along the Satilla River, and for once Mama started right off talking about us. "I want my babies to live the parts of my life that I missed. Do you think that's too much to ask, Ed?"

"We all want the best for our children, Adele."

"Well, I want mine to finish high school before they run off and get married like I did, and I don't want them to live in a mobile home park where they can be blown to bits by a strong wind. The very thought of hurricanes makes me weak."

"You lived in a mobile home?"

"Oh, no." Mama's head turned so fast, her braid whipped around like a tail. "I was just letting my imagination run wild."

"So I take it I shouldn't show you any mobile homes?"

"Not on your life." Mama patted his arm, enjoying him funning with her.

Finally we turned onto a dirt road that ran alongside the water. While "a cottage by the river" sounded like something out of a storybook, this drab white box set on a dirt yard with a couple of straggly cottonwoods was a fishing shack, plain and simple. I could easily imagine it as a set for a horror movie: fun-loving teenagers would drive down this lane, cook hot-dogs by the river, make out on porch swings, hammocks, and mildewed mattresses, and then be killed off one by one. Not only were we as far removed from the wide porches and flower boxes of Union Street as we could get, we had crossed the line into Brantley County.

Adrian dashed from the car, hell-bent on seeing the river. "I expect you to stay right there on the shore, mister," Mama called. "Not one toe in that water; do you hear me?"

Mama was polite about the place, but we could tell it took a lot of effort for her to find something good to say. "Well, it is a charming area, but the river worries me, Ed. It's so close, and my babies are so young."

She went on to talk about hurricanes and storm surges and flood insurance, but by then she had earned Captain Ed's sympathy. "Say no more, Adele." He, too, had his eye on the river, no doubt uneasy about Adrian drowning on his watch. "I understand completely."

The next week, Captain Ed took us to a converted carriage house on Ellis Street, which was right behind Union. We could have walked there in two minutes, but the Captain picked us up as usual and talked the entire three blocks about how Mama would find this place "full of charm."

Doubtful, we followed Mama down a narrow brick walk to the bright blue front door. Adrian stayed right with us because there was no room to run. Captain Ed pointed to brown, overgrown vegetation. "This is good garden space, Adele."

"Oh, my husband loves to garden," Mama chirped. "We could try canning everything we grow, couldn't we, Michaelena?"

I was not interested in canning, and Christina had stopped dead to consider the perfect A-shape of the roofline over the blue door, as if that A was one of those signs Mama always sought and this was the house to make her happy. "Not FNB," I hissed into her ear. "Too small."

Beyond the front door was a narrow staircase leading straight up. To the right was a tiny living room; to the left, an even smaller dining room. "The kitchen is in the back, Adele." Captain Ed led Mama past a table set for four.

Christina, Adrian, and I scrambled up the stairs. We let Adrian reach the top first, one little triumph to keep him peaceable, and peeked into a tidy bathroom with pale lavender towels. On either side of the bathroom were the two bedrooms, each one with slanted ceilings and pastel wallpaper.

Adrian, sometimes quicker than we gave him credit for, took one look and set the record straight. "I'm not sharing a room with you two."

"As if we want you to." I stuck out my tongue.

Mama's voice was high and excited as she called us down to look at the view of live oaks, date palms, oleander, and creeping vines that swirled over the fancy tiled roofs and massive chimneys of the grand house facing Union Street.

"That's not Father Knows Best either," Christina said right out loud.

Mama laughed and tousled Christina's hair. "No, baby, it certainly is not."

Captain Ed took us to Willie's Wee-Nee Wagon to celebrate finding a house Mama liked, not realizing, I guess, what she really liked was the one *behind* the carriage house. We sat at a picnic table and ate hot dogs buried in onions, relish, chili, and sauerkraut. We drank root beer floats while Mama and Captain Ed strolled off to smoke cigarettes. Adrian finished first and trailed after them, but soon returned and wriggled himself in between Christina and me.

"What's your problem?" I asked. His face wore its usual blotchy, sweaty grimace, but his shoulders were slumped and his chin grazed his chest. "You look like someone stuck a pin in you."

"You want the rest of my float?" Christina offered.

He shook his head.

"Adrian, you are such a Mama's baby. Do you have to always be hanging on her?"

"Not now," he said.

Christina and I took one look at each other and flew away from the picnic table.

There in the parking lot Mama stood with one round hip pressed against the Cadillac. She held her cigarette aloft and laughed up into Captain Ed's face. They were so close, we were positive Captain Ed must feel Mama's sweet onion breath blowing against his mustache like the threat of a tropical depression.

No matter how sorely we longed to know everything, seeing Mama with Captain Ed simply added to our life mysteries of why men loved Mama or how fate threw Mama and Daddy together and held them fast while they dreamed their own separate dreams. That day at Willie's Wee-Nee Wagon confirmed that Mama was our axis, the one we all orbited with awe and fascination, and it had become our duty to study her, to watch her close and listen to her stories. Only then, we decided, could the Dunegan family take hold, our small bursts of color shining against the dark in a bright, freeform design.

The Wedding Crasher

Emily Wishart had grown weary of weddings. She was weary from buying shower gifts and wedding gifts and bridesmaids gowns. She was weary from decorating church pews and social halls and honeymoon cars. She was weary from tending to tearful mothers and pinched-looking fathers and hysterical brides. She was weary from eating cleverly flavored wedding cakes and smiling for photographers and being pushed forward to catch bridal bouquets. Most of all, Emily was weary from negotiating with uncooperative bridegrooms, men who seemed perfectly genial until faced with the challenge of selecting reception halls or disc jockeys or silver patterns. "Whatever," they would snap when their brides approached them with glossy brochures. "You decide."

Weddings had put Emily off the idea of marriage, but here she was, once again, shopping at Filene's for a bridal shower gift. After gift buying for six weddings in as many months, Emily knew Filene's housewares by heart. She knew where to look for the codes that matched those printed on the bride's gift list. She knew the asterisks next to an item indicated a sale price. She knew the gregarious, middle-aged salesclerk would be helpful and the soft-spoken, mousy one would not. In fact, Emily had become so adept at finding her way around the linens and crystal and silverware, the pots and pans and small appliances, she told friends that if she were ever held hostage by a crazed cutlery-wielding bride and her life depended on the correct identification of Pfaltzgraff and Dansk china patterns, she would have an excellent chance of survival.

Today's chore would be a breeze, swift and light and calming. She had merely to type the name of her co-worker, Maryelle Johansen, into the bridal registry computer, wait for the pages to print, and then snap up something affordable. Some pieces of stainless flatware, perhaps, or an ovenware bowl, something as plain and practical as Emily herself. But today Emily was distracted, perhaps by the unnecessary blast of air conditioning or the smudgy fingerprints on the computer screen or maybe her own state of wedding weariness, and without conscious thought she typed *Johnson*, the name of an old boyfriend, in place of *Johansen*.

An honest error, really, and easy to correct, but now she discovered herself tapping the screen directly on the square labeled *Groom*. M-A-T-T-H-E-W. She watched her index finger firmly punch each letter.

In another second, the screen filled with five Matthew Johnsons and their perspective brides. She couldn't turn away now. Her eyes scanned the names, looking for—for what? Matt had started dating an Ecology major almost immediately after he had informed Emily that life was short and he was too young for commitment. That girl had been tall and earthy with a name to match. Fern? Tree? Moss?

Obviously Emily had succeeded in excising that small detail from her memory, although she could see that girl as clear as Waterford Crystal right now. She was slender-shouldered and wide-hipped and favored jeans that rode low on her hips and black, ribbed, tank tops. Her hair was the color of pine mulch and it clung to her ordinary, pleasant face as if she were filled with static electricity. Only her eyes were remarkable. Pale and green as peeled grapes, they turned luminous on those rare occasions—usually breakfast in the cafeteria—when Emily spotted her wearing glasses. Bird? Sky? Star?

Now Emily saw that Matt, as square and solid as a rock formation, had joined the girl with the clingy hair and the grape eyes. He wore his usual charcoal gray t-shirt, his usual sloppy jeans, and that droll little twist to his mouth that made his sarcasm charming. There they stood, between the Lenox and the Mikasa, while the girl whispered her preferences and Matt nodded his sleek dark head, agreeing no doubt to buy her the world, but without any intention of carrying it out. Thankfully, by the time Emily correctly entered Maryelle's name and watched the pages print, the mirages were gone.

In spite of her doubts that it would ever be used, Emily bought Maryelle a waffle iron for her wedding next month and a set of woven placemats for her bridal shower in two weeks, items that together exceeded the minimum for free gift wrapping. She waited in line at Gift Wrapping, cowed by her own brief flight of fancy. It had been ten years since her breakup with Matthew Johnson. Had he stayed with the ecology girl after graduation, they would have married long ago, and they would not be living in any metropolitan area along the east coast; they would be living in an Alpine cabin, a tropical beach hut, an English gatehouse, any of those very same places she and Matt had once talked of living.

In spite of her certainty in Matt's life choices, Emily found herself asking the gift wrapper about the Bridal Registry. "If I only know one name, either the bride's or the groom's, how do I know if I have the correct gift list?"

"Do you know the wedding date?" The gift wrapper, a lacquered woman of indeterminate age, was as polished and precise as her craft.

"Fourth of July."

"That will narrow it down." The woman's glazed eyebrows furrowed by a hair or two. "I don't believe the Fourth is on a weekend this year, is it?"

"Probably not. They're known for being unconventional." Emily marveled at the ease of her own fabrication, that quick bright lie that burst from her mouth like a champagne bubble. But really, what else could she say? Years ago, she had spun similar stories to prevent herself from looking foolish. Then she told friends she had broken up with Matt because he had no goals, no sense of purpose, and she could not be wandering around the world aimlessly while he found himself.

"What if they're living out of state?" Emily asked the gift-wrapper now.

"They would still be listed with our affiliates. In most states." The woman deftly unspooled a handful of wide, white ribbon. "You may have to try a larger chain of stores. You know," she said, pausing to make eye contact over the rim of her reading glasses. "I had a niece stationed in Alaska who registered with Wal-Mart."

Wal-Mart.

As fate would have it, Emily did occasionally shop at Wal-Mart to stock up on items like shampoo and vitamins and ink cartridges, and she refused to give up those cost-cutting savings out of fear that an old, dead romance might pop into her head again. Two weeks later, the day after the office bridal shower for Maryelle, Emily was not totally surprised to find herself next to the Wal-Mart jewelry counter, tapping letters onto the Gift Registry computer screen. She closed her eyes and took a deep breath as she waited out the drone of information being retrieved, the furtive act of uncovering personal data that was intended to be made public.

Emily opened her eyes as the screen filled with twelve Matthew Johnsons. Twelve men and their fiancées from all over rural United States. No, two of the listings were for baby gifts and one was for an anniversary. Any of them, Emily realized, could be her Matthew.

She scanned the names of the women, looking for something nature-like. Ivy? Heather? Lily? No, there was nothing there from the plant world. Zero. Zip. Nada. Emily's finger, her carefully manicured, clear-polished forefinger made one lingering sweep, and there it was: Autumn. Not nearly as exotic or earthy as Emily had remembered. Autumn Sands and Matthew Johnson of Spearfish, North Dakota, were to marry, not on July 4th as Emily had guessed, but on the first Saturday in September.

She tapped their names, she pushed the Print button, and she scooped the slips of paper—not full letter-sized pages, but pages the size of cash register receipts—into her bag. Later, after she had made her own purchases and returned to the city, she would consider actually reading them.

Once she had studied her road atlas, Emily had no problem imagining Matt in Spearfish, South Dakota. No problem at all. Spearfish was on the northwest perimeter of the Black Hills. Matt would love that mix of prairie grass and pine glades and granite hills. She could see him now, standing at the edge of a canyon to hear the whistle of wind, to feel the updraft rise against his neck and push his hair skyward, to revel in what he claimed were his Native American bloodlines.

But where had he and Autumn been for the past ten years? Right there on the edge of that canyon? And why had they not married sooner? The gift list from Wal-Mart could not answer that, but maybe it could offer some insights into Matt's present life. Emily laid the three long strips of paper across her kitchen counter like newspaper columns and was disappointed to find that in spite of their length, each slip contained no more than ten gift suggestions. Her insights into Matt's current lifestyle would be limited to less than thirty very ordinary items such as a vacuum, a coffeemaker, and a bathroom scale. Had these people accumulated nothing in their years together? Or had they truly been living abroad, happily ensconced in a seaside Portuguese cottage or in an airy apartment at the edge of the Black Forest? How would they have supported themselves all that time?

Emily was fascinated by a few items. The twelve-piece tool set was a surprise as Matt had never been adept at repairs. In their three years together at college, his car was always in the shop, and it had been up to Emily to drive them anywhere off-campus. The card table and folding chairs offered another puzzle. Try as she might, Emily could not visualize Matt and the ecology girl anywhere near a card table, let alone playing cards. Card games, Matt always said, were for children.

Emily was amused and annoyed by the requests for items in the Froggy's Pond decor. Maybe she could accept the lamb's wool Rainforest rug (the most expensive item on the lists) and the kitchen items from the Garden Collection, but little green frogs? Really now. The best items, the ones that made her outright smile, were for a tent and *one* sleeping bag. Matt had loved the outdoors, and every weekend he could borrow a car, they traded days off from their summer jobs (his a lifeguard at the Fitchburg Municipal Pool; hers a counselor at Camp Haven on Lake Ontario) to meet at some equidistant point, Vermont or New Hampshire or the Adirondacks, and camp under the summer stars. Driving all those hours to cook over a fire (hot dogs or low-grade hamburgers that sizzled down to the size of a quarter) and sleep on the unyielding ground in her brother's musty Boy Scout tent had been the most romantic thing Emily had ever done. Did Matt remember those times as well? She ran her finger over COLEMAN 5LB SLP BAG. Did this mean Matt would now camp alone?

On Saturdays Emily bought groceries and did laundry and had dinner with friends. On Sundays she cooked, on Sunday nights she watched the weather channel and planned her wardrobe for the week, and on Monday mornings she was good to go. Nothing disturbed her worknight sleep patterns. From the time her head hit the pillow at ten o'clock until she awoke every morning at six, she slept the sleep of the dead. This Sunday began the same. She made vegetable soup and eggplant parmesan, dishes that would last her most of the week. She read the Sunday paper and called her mother. In between rain showers, she took a long walk and thought about Matt and his clingy-haired bride. The mystery of what they had done and where they had been for the past ten years had taken on new importance. What if they had *not* been together? What if Matt had been single all that time, or worse yet, what if he had been looking for Emily and was simply marrying Autumn now because she was convenient?

Emily returned to her apartment and dug through the garbage, the morning's discard of onionskins and potato peelings and scarred tomato pieces, until she found the gift lists. She wiped them clean and took one more look. Maybe Matt and his bride-to-be wanted to live simply. Maybe a card table and folding chairs were all that would fit into their teensy apartment or their camper or their rented room. Maybe they requested only one sleeping bag because that was all that was necessary. They *preferred* to sleep that close together.

Emily stood at the kitchen counter a long time and then, as dusk settled on the Sunday-quiet streets, she sat at her own two-person table and turned on her green globed lamp. The Matthew she had known would be perfectly content with a card table and sleeping bag. He believed in living as simply as possible. No baggage for him when a sleeping bag and the contents of his backpack would serve any need he may have. But that Matthew would have never agreed to a wedding ceremony that involved guests and gifts and unnecessary *things*.

After ten years, she imagined him saying, *why marry?*

So the new Matthew, the one who had agreed to marry and become domestic, the one who would now accept gifts and publicly declare his intentions at some sort of official occasion, that Matthew would also have agreed to receive more *things* than were listed at Wal-Mart. Obviously, Emily concluded, there were more lists at other stores.

After a sleepless night, Emily spent her Monday morning at work searching for online bridal registries. She tried Sears and Penneys and K-Mart, stores that might be plentiful in South Dakota. Nothing. She tried TJMaxx and Target and Pier One. Nothing. She tried Kohl's and Crate & Barrel. Nothing. Oh, there were dozens and dozens of Matthew Johnsons, but none of them were marrying Autumn Sands in Spearfish, South Dakota. The only list in existence was the very one Emily had found with one trip to the suburbs. Thirty items from Wal-Mart appeared to be the sum extent of Matt and Autumn's earthly needs.

Somehow, now on an internet roll, Emily found herself checking flights to Rapid City. Because the first Saturday of September was also Labor Day weekend, flights were double their every-other-day-of-the-month rate. What a shame. She started to hit the back key, to gracefully exit this little game of fantasy, when her practical nature fell prey to something resembling regret. Wasn't this just like her, it said, to let dollar signs block the way to her heart? When did she ever spend her hard-earned salary on anything but necessities? And wasn't it her own dutiful complacency that had so easily let Matthew go?

Okay, she had said to Matt all those years ago, *if that's the way you feel.* When she had wanted to say *no, of course I won't let you leave me because the ecology girl wants you. I will follow you to the ends of the earth until you come to your senses.* She had taken the easy way out. Anything to avoid a swarming, throbbing, sweet and sticky mess, a beehive that love had dropped and shattered in her path.

Without conscious thought, Emily's credit card was in her hand and her flight confirmation was sliding into the printer tray. For good measure, she booked a rental car as well. Now what? Clothes, of course. She would need something less business-like than her work clothes and something more presentable than her worn jeans and loose, woven shirts. And a gift. No one would dare refuse admittance to wedding crashers bearing gifts.

In the weeks leading up to the wedding, Emily had no second thoughts —not one—and she told no one of her plans, even when she was tempted. "You look great, Emily," her friends said. "Are you seeing someone?"

"Not exactly." Ordinarily Emily could fabricate small details to ease her way through awkward situations, but she was not at all comfortable with lying. Lies were necessary, she maintained, only when the truth was too difficult to be told.

"I'm spending Labor Day with friends on the Cape," Emily heard herself tell her mother.

"Which friends are those?" her mother asked.

"People from work." Emily felt guilt push into her throat. "Not really friends."

She stayed late each night to complete her work projects in advance, and on weekends she went shopping. She wanted to look good, naturally, but she did not want anything too fussy or anything that would wrinkle the moment she sat down. She settled on a simple, black sleeveless that was not linen, but would stand up to those scorching temperatures that apparently plagued South Dakota in the summer. On a whim, she bought amazingly high-heeled sandals to go with it.

The wedding gift took a little more thought. Her personal favorite was obviously the single sleeping bag, but she did not want to lug anything so large and bulky with her. She refused to buy anything with a frog on it, and so, in the end, she settled on a simple but expensive silver cake knife that had nothing to do with the Wal-Mart list. Boxed and wrapped, it would fit neatly into her single piece of luggage. For the wedding, she could easily carry it in her purse.

The weekend before Labor Day, she went to her usual salon for a long overdue cut and color and then splurged on a facial and manicure as well.

"Special occasion?" asked the girls in the salon.

"A wedding," Emily answered. "The wedding of an old friend in South Dakota."

"Wouldn't you know," said Rosa the manicurist. "Old friends always have weddings in the most inconvenient places."

Emily told her she didn't mind in the slightest. It would be nice to escape to the countryside, to have a change of scene.

"Will you do that when you marry?" asked Rosa. "Where will you have your wedding, do you think?"

Emily was taken aback. It had been so long since someone had assumed she might actually marry that at first she could think of nothing to say. Then, quite easily, she recalled all the plans she and Matt had once made. "An island wedding might be nice," Emily said, "with only immediate family." She imagined their backs to the ocean, their faces toward the sun and the breezy white canopy shading their guests: her parents, his parents, her brother, his brother, people they knew only through photographs.

"Maybe an elopement would be better," she said, as she remembered another of Matt's suggestions. "To Paris. Or Venice." Matt always thought an intimate ceremony in a gondola might be over the top. *Over the top.* She had forgotten how often he used that phrase. No matter what Matt planned, he wanted it to be "over the top," something distinctive and daring and totally unlike anything anyone else they might know would do.

Could that be the reason, Emily wondered, why he would choose to marry in Spearfish, North Dakota?

There *were* moments leading up to her day of departure when the word *foolish* fluttered in Emily's brain. Or sometimes *pathetic* sounded like a small, dim bell. What was it she hoped to accomplish by this extravagant act? Nothing at all, she told herself. She was simply curious to learn the way her life *might* have gone. And what was it she planned to say—as she worked her way down the receiving line, for example? Again, nothing. She figured no one in attendance was likely to recognize the new Emily, who was a good ten pounds thinner, who wore glasses instead of contacts, and who wore her hair short and dyed a rich red mahogany. Matt was the only one who might know her immediately, and there was nothing to be said to him. Her satisfaction would come from simply being, from observing and being observed. Let him draw his own conclusions. Her presence would be, in Matthew's own words, "over the top."

Emily's only small, niggling concern was that she had no idea where or at what hour the wedding was being held. But how many weddings in the whole of Spearfish (population 7000, according to Wikipedia) could there be on that same Saturday? Upon landing in Rapid City, she retrieved her one piece of luggage, which could have served as a carry-on if it had not been for the cake knife, and went to the car rental desk. There standing in line directly in front of her was Matthew Johnson, solid and real and completely alone.

"Matt?"

He turned and smiled with only a trace of annoyance. "Mark," he said.

"Pardon me?"

"I'm Mark." His dark eyebrows lifted in a familiar way, and Emily wondered if he might be speaking in code.

"Don't worry," he said, "I'm not *too* ashamed to be confused with my big brother. Are you here for the wedding?"

It took a moment for the man's words to settle into her consciousness.

"Yes." Her voice was soft and tentative, so she tried again with conviction. "Yes. I am."

"Good thing I ran into you." For another half a second, she wanted to believe this very familiar man truly was Matt and he meant every word he said. "The wedding's been changed from Bridal Veil Falls to Roughlock Falls. On the other side of Savoy, do you know it?"

Emily nodded, further convinced there was a code involved.

"Too many guests for the first site." Matt's double was amused. "The whole thing kind of got out of hand. Some joker even registered them with Wal-Mart; did you hear about that?"

The line shifted forward then and this Matthew double, so innocent, so unknowing, so unaware of who Emily was and what she meant to the real Matthew Johnson, stepped up to the counter.

Although tempted to follow, Emily stayed behind, prepared to wait her turn.

Saturday morning was humid and overcast, which Emily figured was better than clear skies and a hot sun beating down on her fair shoulders and face. Knowing her dress and high-heeled sandals were far from practical for an outdoor ceremony, Emily wore them anyway. No one here today would know her, and she may as well look good as she stood alone along the edge of the canyon, a spectator on the sidelines of life. She drove south on Main Street, where the first sign marked the turn for the Spearfish Canyon Scenic Highway: **Matt and Autumn <This Way**. Their names were printed in pink and encased in a heart. So bizarre. There was a second sign at the Bridal Veil Falls, a trickle of waterfall along the side of the road, and a third in Savoy, where she was directed to turn right onto a dirt road that seemed to go on forever.

By the time she reached the parking lot, Emily was feeling queasy. She double-checked her purse for the cake knife, noting how insignificant it looked in its wedding white wrappings. How had she ever thought it could gain her proper entry? Well, if any of the true invited guests asked how she fit into this occasion, maybe Emily would simply have to tell them. "I brought Matt and Autumn together," Emily might be tempted to say. "I am personally responsible for them being joined in marriage today."

The people emerging from the parked cars wore picnic clothes, summer print sundresses and Birkenstocks, denim shorts and sleeveless tops, khaki shorts and plaid shirts. Emily teetered along at a discreet distance, kicking up gritty soil that filled her sandals and coated the hem of her black dress like rust. There were other signs, official signs that pointed out the picnic area and the trail to the falls, but Emily followed Matt's guests straight ahead, over the bridge spanning a musical creek. There they gathered, each of them greeting one another with the hearty exclamations of people who had been distant for a long time. They were oblivious to Emily, who stood transfixed by the sheer grandeur of water tumbling over the rocky walls of the canyon. Matt had actually found the perfect place for his wedding. What could Paris or Venice or an ordinary beach have offered someone who detested anything too obviously pretentious? Grand, but natural, that was his style.

Upon the arrival of a man in a gray suit, the guests merged into an orderly arrangement that faced the falls. Emily recognized Matt's parents, although they looked older and more out of sorts than they had in snapshots. The man in the suit, whom Emily guessed to be a justice of the peace rather than a preacher, and Mark, Matt's lookalike brother, stood at attention with their backs to the falls. A recording of Handel's Water Music began to play and a woman wearing a pale green dress and carrying a bouquet of Queen Anne's Lace and cabbage roses crossed the bridge and joined Mark. The color of her hair and the shape of her eyes easily identified her as Autumn's sister.

As the bride and groom crossed the bridge and passed through the guests, Emily became filled with dismay at her own foolishness. She had wasted a great deal of money and two perfectly good vacation days to

48

come to the wedding of a stranger. Autumn Sands was the same girl she had known from college, all right. Emily recognized the same narrow shoulders, the same slender throat above the scooped neckline, the same broad hips that filled out the skirt of her slim eyelet dress. Autumn had not changed a wink, right down to the hair that wound from her crown of wildflowers and clung to her face, but this man she was about to marry was not the same Matthew Johnson Emily herself had once loved. This Matthew Johnson was large and balding with a full face and a gold stud in his left earlobe. The Matthew Johnson she had known would never wear anything like those shiny black slacks and that tailored white shirt. This Matthew Johnson resembled nothing so much as a well-fed waiter.

And then he spoke and it was her Matthew's own voice that welcomed them to this special occasion, this day of love and celebration. "Rejoice with us, dear friends." The words caught Emily off guard. Her Matt would have been more direct. He would have said, "Hey, glad to have you with us. No party is complete without good friends." He would have made eye contact as he spoke and not let his eyes drift over her and the other guests in such a pontifical manner.

Speaking above the rush of the falls, the bridal couple recited their vows. There was no mention of honor or obedience or how long they both shall live. "I love you," they declared to each other before the man in the suit pronounced them man and wife.

The guests applauded and sighed.

"Absolutely lovely," said the woman next to Emily.

Had Emily thought beyond this moment, her plan would have included a hasty exit, one in which, her mission accomplished, she would simply walk directly over the bridge to the parking lot and drive away. Now it was too late, and she was caught up in events that she had neither expected nor planned to avoid. She did not expect the newlyweds to publicly invite all those present to a reception at the nearby lodge and restaurant. She did not expect them to drift easily into the crowd, shaking hands and kissing cheeks as they accepted congratulations. She did not expect a masculine hand to reach from behind and take her elbow.

The hand belonged to a man her own age, an ordinary man with short, brown hair and wearing jeans, a white dress shirt with cuffs rolled to his elbows, and a tie with whales on it. "I know I should remember you," he said.

"Really?" She had never seen this man before in her life.

"Maybe we went to college together?"

Emily smiled, amused by his persistence.

"At Penn State?"

She took a closer look. The only truly distinctive thing about him was his square-framed glasses, but the laugh lines around his mouth *might* be familiar. That and the high color along his cheekbones.

"I'm Greg Lydell." He offered his hand. "I was Matt's college roommate."

"I'm Emily Wishart." She shook his hand. "I was Matt's college girlfriend. His *first* college girlfriend."

"Emily." He shook harder. "I knew it was you. You look great."

"Thanks."

"So Matt is finally taking the big step." Greg grinned in disbelief. "Autumn has the patience of a saint. I'll say that much for her."

Emily was tempted to say that she too had the patience of a saint, that she too would have waited ten years to marry Matthew—the old Matthew—but now Greg was talking about how fast the years had gone by.

"Doesn't it seem like yesterday that we were all in college together, hanging out in that unbelievably bad apartment behind the pizza place?"

"Matt's place?"

"I thought it was Autumn's place."

Not at first, Emily wanted to say. In the beginning, that cramped, dingy space, which was made bearable by the smell of baking dough and tomato sauce, had been Matt's alone. Staying there on the nights when Matt's buddies and their girlfriends had cleared out in search of a better party, Emily imagined she could be living inside a loaf of bread, where everything was spongy underfoot, but mere breathing offered a pleasant high.

"Matt and Autumn still live in State College. Hard to believe, isn't it?"

It *was* hard to believe. Greg began to talk about "life after college," about grad school and jobs and the cost of living in large cities, but Emily's mind was stuck on the thought of Matt and Autumn living exactly where she had last seen them. How could that be? What had happened to those faraway adventures Matt spun night after night as they lay in that musty tent—or on that narrow bed where a thin wall separated them from the pizza oven?

"Why did they come here to be married?" she interrupted Greg's unhappy tale of lost investments. "I know it's spectacular, but how did they find it?" Emily had a brief, fleeting image of Matt and Autumn, backpacks slung from their heaving shoulders as they climbed up from the gorge and vowed to make this the site of their nuptials.

"Matt's brother suggested it. It's a cool destination, you know?"

Matt's *brother*?

Emily sensed the newlyweds drawing nearer. Their greetings and the laughter of the guests were building, growing closer, and while Matt had changed both too much and too little to have an effect on her now, Emily desperately wanted to avoid Autumn. Autumn would know exactly who Emily was, and she would obviously assume that Matt had invited her. Such a prospect had never crossed Emily's mind until this very moment.

"Something wrong?" Greg leaned in close and spoke quietly.

"I shouldn't be here." Emily glanced over her shoulder to see Autumn as purposefully headed in their direction as a missile locked on a target. "I wasn't invited," she whispered before Matt, cheerfully oblivious, barreled his way past Autumn with all the grace of a steamroller.

"Hey, man." Matt crunched Greg's shoulders together in a mighty squeeze. "How the hell have you been?" He loosened his collar. Rivulets of sweat ran from his receding hairline and glistened like sun on the river. His eyes were exactly as Emily remembered, dark and flickery, always looking beyond what was immediately before him.

"Hey, Babe," Matt said when he noticed her. "God, I haven't seen you in a lifetime." He moved quickly for a large man, and when Emily opened her mouth to make some banal, proper response, he drew her to him and kissed her.

Had she imagined this reaction from Matt, she might also have imagined a reaction from herself, a deep and painful stirring, perhaps, or a great rush of regret, some response worthy of a romance novel at the least. Instead, the thought that crashed into her head like a stone sliding from the canyon wall was simple and stark and true. She could be anyone, any other woman Matt might have known, a fellow student or a co-worker or a distant cousin. She was no longer the girl who lent him her car or drove hours to camp by his side or let him go when he fell in love. She was not a fond memory, but a far distant one, familiar only in a pleasantly vague way.

Autumn, meanwhile, had wrapped her long thin arms around Greg. "I knew you would make the trip." Her kiss left a coppery smudge on Greg's cheek. "I'm so happy you're here." She spun to face Emily. "Do I know you?" Her eyes narrowed to pale green slits and her shiny, sienna lips puckered in concentration.

"This is my friend Emily," Greg said with a convincing hum. "From Boston."

Emily knew she did not deserve to be rescued. She deserved to be humiliated, scorned, publicly stoned, all those things she had wished for Matt as punishment for leaving her. She deserved to hear whatever Autumn might say to the woman who had taken the easy way out and now had the nerve to show up on her hard-earned wedding day. All these years of living with a difficult Matt must have outfitted Autumn not only with the patience of a saint but the devotion of a disciple, the tenacity of a redwood. Was that the same thing as love?

"What a beautiful wedding." Emily offered her hand. "A perfect wedding," she said, and she meant it.

"Emily." Autumn gave the same emphasis to each syllable, as if recalling an important historical fact. "I had no idea you and Greg were back together. You were such a darling couple in college." She went on a bit more, recalling specific events, a party in a dairy barn, a drive to the shore, a night of drunken hi-jinks, none of which Emily had ever been a part of. "We had some wild times together, didn't we?"

"We did." Emily nodded, considering all she had missed. She turned back to Matthew. He was bouncing on his toes in his eagerness to move on to other guests, and Emily recognized all that had passed and all that had changed and all that had been lost for Matthew since she let him go. For a man who had dreamed big, he had lived little.

"So, I'll see you two at the reception," Matt insisted. "We need to catch up."

Emily nodded, but her mind was elsewhere, her heart free and flying—hovering over Paris and Venice and moonlit beaches and all those places for which she had longed, those places far beyond this rocky river's edge where at last the sun was burning through the clouds of a very ordinary late summer afternoon.

Storytelling

My sister disappeared right after Kent State. Swept from the face of the earth, my mother said, as she told her story over and over to anyone who would listen. Searching for Suzanne had become her life's work. Before that day, her life had been raising her girls, me and Suzanne. And before that, for however short a time, we had been a family. My mother could have had no intuition that as we decreased in number, her work would become greater and her stories more numerous.

My father died when I was ten and Suzanne almost six. He had a massive coronary on the courthouse steps after delivering his closing argument in defense of Marlene Gibson, acquitted the next day of murdering her husband. My mother, afraid she would sicken and die and leave us orphans, became a hypochondriac after his death. She read medical journals and stockpiled prescription bottles, and every night, like a bedtime story, she told us about the dangers of the world.

These dangers were endless and everywhere. In the house we were to keep our hands away from the mangle, our forks out of the toaster, and our transistor radios away from the bathtub. In the street we were to avoid speeding cars, slow-moving cars with male drivers, and anyone asking for directions or offering candy. If Suzanne and I were traumatized by any of this, we soon shook it off by inventing our own stories. "What would you do if Mr. Mariani offered us some Good 'n Plenty?" I'd whisper after my mother kissed us good night, smoothing our hair and whispering sadly how much she loved us.

"Tell him we'd rather have Almond Joys." We giggled. Mr. Mariani owned the corner grocery and yelled if we didn't close the lid of the ice cream freezer all the way.

"What if Mr. Lehman offered us a ride?"

"Tell him we won't ride in a pile of junk." Mr. Lehman was our principal at Lockwood Elementary and no more threatening than his dilapidated Ford pickup.

Later, as Suzanne curled against my back and sucked her thumb, I thought about the stories that did frighten me. Accidents of nature, my mother called them: tornadoes that sucked Dorothy out of Kansas, lightning bolts that could find me whether I was in an open field or under a tree, flood waters that spilled banks and crossed bridges and could carry me away down the Ohio to the Mississippi and the ocean beyond. I worried long after Suzanne fell asleep about accidents of nature.

At first, when we tried to piece together that day at Kent Sate, there were other students who remembered Suzanne walking with them as they left the campus, sent into that spring day with whatever they could carry, like refugees from a war-torn city. But when we watched the films taken by a Cleveland news crew, we couldn't find her. It was impossible to identify any of the bobbing faces that surged toward the camera, their arms raised in grief or anger or fear, their feet stirring up the dusty residue of winter's grit so they seemed to float on a cloud, an aura of gray to protect them from the newly green farmland they passed.

Callie, a ditzy creature who claimed to be Suzanne's best friend, swore she had been there right along. "But Buzz and I took the road to Aurora, Mrs. Windber," she told my mother, "and Suze stayed with the rest."

We never discovered who "the rest" were, but we learned Callie and Buzz lived off campus and had no real purpose to be on the road to Aurora or anywhere else. They were simply caught up in the spirit of the moment. "It seemed like the right thing to do," Callie said.

My mother always said Suzanne was too easy. "Too eager to please boys" was how she put it. She blamed my father for dying, for leaving us without "an appropriate male influence." Maybe she was right, because Suzanne grew up thinking boys were totally desirable.

Boys were not easily pleased, Suzanne told me. Unlike girlfriends who shared their lunches or lent their jewelry just for the asking, boys insisted she earn whatever she wanted from them through barter, trickery, or an act of bravery. The summer after our father died, Suzanne broke her arm because Terry Planeski dared her to climb the dead apple tree between his house and ours. Shy and apologetic, he was the first one to sign her cast, and she immediately declared it had been worth it.

When Suzanne was thirteen, she told me she played post office during lunch hour in the courtyard off the cafeteria. She and the other brown baggers had more time because they did not have to go through the serving line.

"How does that work?" I asked, hoping for something reasonable.

"The girls count off and when a boy calls our number we go behind the fountain with him." She was matter-of-fact, pulling at the sheer pink curtain my mother had looped over our bedposts as a makeshift canopy.

"Then what do you do?" I crossed my arms and waited her out.

"Jimmy Betts kisses, but the rest stand there and act stupid, tell dirty jokes." She waved with scorn, her dark eyes solemn and defiant. "When I go back to the benches with the other girls, I never tell. Even when Mike Granta said we French kissed, I pretended we did."

For all her willingness, Suzanne had few dates in high school. Maybe her eagerness scared them off or maybe she could no longer find anyone to challenge her. She spent weekends running with her girlfriends and evenings watching television with our mother.

When I was home from college, she told me about boys she liked, but mostly hung around with me and John Redinger, my longtime boyfriend. She flirted with him and asked outrageous questions.

"Does it hurt the first time for a boy, too, John?" We were at the Dairy Queen, and she propped her chin on her hand and leaned across her banana split.

John never missed a beat. "Excruciatingly, Suzanne," he said as he spooned hot fudge into his mouth.

When the news magazines splashed the photo of the girl kneeling over the dying boy, Suzanne was there in the background, closer to the trees. And when well-meaning friends said the figure we claimed as Suzanne was interchangeable with any other young woman who had long dark hair and a green headband, I pointed to the slacks she wore. They were a distinctive green print which, when seen close at hand, was an intricate blend of flowers embossed by a slender gold thread. They were my slacks, the new ones I had been missing since Suzanne visited us in Boardman at spring break.

The sudden notion that Suzanne had chosen to disappear, leaving my mother heartbroken and taking my new slacks with her, burned furiously in my brain from that moment on. Even when, in the light of what developed, my anger seemed justified, it gave me no solace. This was one story Suzanne had chosen not to share with me, and I was certain that in some way, I had failed her.

When the dorms were unsealed for the Kent students to claim their belongings and make arrangements to complete the semester's work, Mom and I went to Fletcher Hall to get Suzanne's things. No one had heard of her. We were shuffled from office to office in Taylor Hall before a woman carrying a salmon-colored card came over to us.

Suzanne Windber, she told us, had withdrawn eighteen months ago, in the middle of her sophomore year. She tapped the card with her pencil. Suzanne's mailing address had been off-campus, not Fletcher Hall.

We got the address from the woman before we left. The paper, with KSU embossed across the top, shook in my mother's hand. "I guess it could be worse," she said as we walked to the car with our eyes averted from the parking lot and the grassy knoll just beyond.

Callie opened the door at the Water Street apartment as if she'd been expecting us. "Hey, great to see you. Come on in. Any word on Suze?"

My mother, always one for social niceties, could not shape the words to respond.

"Tell us what you know, Callie." I moved to the plaid sofa and pulled my mother down beside me, an announcement we were prepared to wait.

"All right." Callie dragged a kitchen chair across the bare pine floor and sat facing us. Her platinum hair, almost the color and texture of a dandelion gone to seed, reached to her elbows. Her bare legs were freckled and long and she pulled the tails of her oversized work shirt down over them as she talked. Slowly at first, then very quickly. "Well, we all moved here about two years ago. In August, I think."

"Who's 'we'?"

"Me and Buzz. Con and Suze." She said "Con-and-Suze" as if she were speaking of one person. "Suze didn't come 'til school started though."

Callie kept talking, her pale eyes following some tempo in her head as she struggled with chronological order. I could feel her eagerness to please, to perform well, to make us feel better. "Then she and Con moved in with some of his friends, closer to campus. We saw them around all the time. I didn't know she'd dropped out." Callie leaned toward my mother, her palms up, asking for forgiveness.

My mother's glasses had slipped below the bridge of her nose, but she didn't bother to push them back. "When did you find out Suzanne was no longer enrolled?"

"Not until that guy came around here the other day looking for Con again."

"What guy, Callie?" I spoke softly and put my hand on her wrist, unable to watch her pull on her shirttails one more time.

She looked puzzled. "The FBI guy that's always looking for Con. Hasn't he found you yet? He knows all about Suze."

Callie was right. Over the next few years FBI Agent Leon Metzer became a regular visitor to our house on Glenwood Avenue, the stucco and brick bought by our father on a G.I. Loan. Metzer had graying hair and startling blue eyes. Formal and taciturn, he warmed up a bit with my mother. She took him through the house as if he would find the sole clue we all needed. She pointed out the swing in the backyard that Suzanne and I had fought over, the kitchen table where we brought boys for her lasagna, and the large sunroom where we had birthday parties and our father's wake.

"There was a time," she often said, "when I could not imagine any greater grief than losing my Nick. I guess I was wrong."

Metzer nodded, following her into the knotty pine den where we now spent our days waiting for Suzanne to return. Metzer was hot and cold in his determination to find her. He admitted he was more interested in finding Con, who was AWOL from the Navy. The fact that Suzanne was with him made her an accomplice or an accessory, but less urgent to be found.

My mother grew dependent on those visits from Leon Metzer. For a while, he suspected Con and Suzanne were involved in other campus demonstrations with violent acts. He gave my mother hope that Suzanne was still alive, at the least. At the most, he gave her someone to talk to, someone with authority, a co-conspirator in her search. My mother fed him her apple strudel or berry pies and called him Leon.

I always suspected Suzanne's case had been shelved and that Leon came only out of courtesy to my mother. At some point, he lost track of Con or lost interest in Suzanne and came by less frequently. My mother became frail. She spent the rest of her life writing letters. Heads of state, talk show hosts, community action groups, the parents of the dead Kent State students, anyone she thought might have an axe to grind received her plea for help in uncovering whatever conspiracy had taken her daughter from her.

I married John Redinger two years after Kent State. He had waited all that time so Suzanne could be my maid-of-honor, and our wedding didn't sit well with my mother. "Your sister will be so disappointed," she told me. "It's something you've planned since you were little girls."

I tried to make it up to her by convincing John we should move in with her until we had money for a house of our own. I assured him it couldn't be any worse than living in one of those new apartment units off Midlothian. They were so poorly constructed and noisy, I told him.

My mother loved the idea of having a man under her roof, someone who praised her cooking and ate everything she put on the table. She didn't pry into our financial affairs, as I feared she might, or offer any advice. Her lifetime ritual of "early to bed, early to rise" left us alone after nine o'clock in the evenings. It could have been the ideal situation except for my sudden change in sleep patterns.

John and I slept in the same four poster bed I'd had since childhood. The same bed where Suzanne and I played dolls, using quilt squares as the boundaries of our kingdom. The same bed where we told our stories and where, until we were teenagers, we had slept together.

Now night after night, I sat bolt upright, and, still in some distant dream state, started to scream. John, sweet and befuddled, talked me down. His sleep-deepened voice calmed me, brought me back to awareness that I was there in his arms and Suzanne was gone. "This is not going to work," I told him, wiping my face on his t-shirt sleeve. "She's still controlling every situation."

We moved out after Aunt Cecelia, my father's sister, agreed to move in. Cecelia was a talker, good company most of the time, and always eager to drive my mother anywhere she wanted to go, but there were times when their relationship wore thin. "I wish I had my house back," my mother said more than once. "Cecelia's a good soul, but I miss the quiet."

By the time John and I bought our own house, an older two-story on the Canfield Road, I was pregnant, due in April. My mother received the news with mixed emotions, as if she could not experience a new child until the old one was accounted for. By the holidays, that agonizing stretch of time when joy seems like a curse, she began to plan for her grandchild, asking about names and imagining what she could cook or knit for this baby.

The second Saturday in February my mother fell on the ice and broke her hip. She was on her way to get the mail, still expectant that someday word from Suzanne would be there. Hidden by the tangle of barberry thorns, she lay there for some time before the neighbor saw her, long enough for complications to develop and lead to her death from pneumonia a week later. Our grief was compounded by guilt. I had been late shopping, John had being working on the house, Cecelia had been at her son's. One of us should have prevented it.

I called Leon Metzer before the funeral to ask if there had been anything new, any small lead that might locate Suzanne before my mother was put to rest. He hesitated. "No, there's been nothing for years, not since they were believed to be in San Francisco with a religious cult."

"But none of your people actually saw Suzanne, actually talked to her?"

"No."

I started to thank him for the kind attention he had given my mother, but he cut me off. "Just doing my job." He sounded gruff. "And I'll tell you something. Don't take up where your mother left off. You don't want your sister back now."

Callie came to the funeral, although I didn't know her at first. Her bobbed hair and added weight gave her a matronly air, but the curious cadence of her words was immediately identifiable. "What a shame about your mother. I saw her obituary in *The Vindicator*." She clasped me to her tweed coat, which smelled like cigarettes and Chanel. "Especially after losing Suze, too."

She asked about John and my pregnancy, but there was nothing new for either of us to say about Suzanne. We paused, wanting another angle to consider, another speck of hope to take with us. "I live in Youngstown now," she said as she left. "I'll keep in touch."

No other mourners mentioned Suzanne. She had become more a bizarre embarrassment than a tragedy. A cross between a deserting husband and a serial killer.

"She killed your mother, you know," Aunt Cecelia said when I sat down. "This whole business just broke her heart, and it was all so unnecessary. Your mother would have accepted any explanation. Anything. But to give none, to never call her. There's no excuse for such behavior. Always was a selfish child. What did I expect?"

When our daughter was born, I named her Susannah, a name that represented the last compromise between my mother and me. Had she been a boy she would have been Nicholas, after my father. We called her Sannah, and I rejoiced that she had none of Suzanne's physical features. She was fair and petite and calm, and while I grieved my mother had not lived to see her, it was an honest grief, at least.

I wasn't ready to let go of my mother's house. It was the only place Suzanne knew to return to. I spent all spring in those rooms, parking Sannah and her carrier in a sunlit spot on the floor and going through every shelf, every drawer. Inch by inch I worked my way through my parents' marriage, my childhood, Suzanne's childhood, all our lives.

"You've got to let go of all this," John warned every morning when he left for work. "You're going to drive yourself into the ground."

"It's going to turn around for me," I promised.

Sannah's eyes, now turning from granite to azure, watched my movement from bookcase to box, from drawer to trashcan. I was methodical and ruthless. I saved my parents' keepsakes, most of my own, and all of Suzanne's. I sold everything that held no depth, that touched no chords. I put Suzanne's things in the attic closet and locked its door, as if on the proverbial skeleton. I arranged to have the house cleaned and then rented it on a long-term lease. I walked away. It was still there, but I didn't have to worry about it.

As Sannah grew, I told her stories, stories I had once told to Suzanne. We trip-trapped like goats and ran, ran like gingerbread boys and acted like monkeys who had stolen the peddler's caps. She was slight and golden and laughed easily; she was nothing like her namesake.

When Jim Jones and his cult died in Guyana, I found myself studying news footage and magazine photos once more. This time I wasn't looking for a familiar piece of clothing. It was more like sifting through ashes for a bright stone, lost from its setting.

I found Callie's name in the phone book. "Tell me about my sister," I said when she answered. "Tell me what she was like."

Again Callie reacted without surprise, as if she'd been expecting my call. "She was . . . not easy, you know." Her words, jerking with fits and starts, were carefully chosen. "She'd buy food and cook elaborate meals for us. She loved that. Then, when she'd flunked her psych test or had a check bounce, she'd hold those fancy dinners against us. She'd threaten to move out. Or she'd lock herself in the bedroom and not let Con near her."

"What about him?"

"Con?" She took a deep breath and blew against the mouthpiece. "He was a sweet guy. Messed up, but sweet. He was real good with her, but he had his problems. I don't expect they were together long after they left, you know?"

"Maybe."

"She could have been there though. With that guy in Guyana. Isn't that why you called?"

"I guess it is." Sannah came toward me carrying one of Suzanne's Golden Books. *The Three Little Kittens.* "Thanks, Callie."

John and I stood in the empty house on Glenwood, waiting for the realtor and watching Sannah run across the hardwood floors. "I put your sister's boxes in the van," John said. "We can store them as long as you like."

Our daughter attempted a pirouette and fell against my leg, laughing. "Come with me, Sannah, and I'll show you a doll that belonged to a little girl who could act just as silly as you do."

"Is the little girl coming here, too?"

"Not today." Someday I would tell her, and her brothers or sisters, stories about Suzanne, the little girl who made mud pies for her father, served them on the rose-patterned cake plate from her tea set, and then cried in outrage when he only pretended to eat them. Later, I would add stories of the ten year old who dared me to walk across the clothesline in the backyard and then refused to speak to me for a week after our mother caught her with one foot on the line, one on the top of the ladder. I would describe the pretty, dark-haired teenager who could twirl fire batons and beat boys at arm wrestling in the cafeteria, the same young woman who left home to follow a star we couldn't see, and became lost on the way back.

I'd make it sound like it turned out okay.

Discrepancies of Love

Our Daddy was a handsome, easygoing man who let life happen to him. Life being Mama and his first wife, Lucille. Daddy had no clue that women expected him to act as good as he looked. They wanted a true prince, a strong savior, a smooth talker, a keen listener, a resourceful provider. Our Daddy was none of those things, although he did rescue our Mama when she was no more than a girl hitchhiking along Route 6 at the Ohio-Pennsylvania state line.

Mama loved to tell that story. "By the time we made it to the far side of Ohio," she always said, "I was ready to follow your Daddy back to Brunswick, Georgia, and stay with him forever." She slid her hand over Daddy's and slipped his cigarette from between his fingers and into her own. "This man was an answer to my prayers."

Daddy never talked about Lucille, who took his kids and all of his money and moved to North Georgia, but my sister Christina grew tearful wondering how it was possible to love someone so much and then so easily let go. "What if Daddy's other wife comes back? What if she brings her kids?" Her words were soft and blubbery, a signal she was fixing to cry loud and long while Daddy's Other Family flickered through her head like a sad movie. "Where are those kids, Michaelena?"

"They grew up and are living happily ever after, Christina, so don't cry about it, okay?"

Our Mama was easy about leaving us with Daddy for weeks at a time while she went off to do good deeds. Not that Daddy didn't *want* to take care of us; it was more a case of Daddy being too sad, too set adrift from Mama's exodus, to function. Without Mama, Daddy grew quiet and soft. Without Mama, Daddy couldn't bear to sleep in their bed. We'd find him on the couch in the morning, the bluish light from the television turning his unshaven face into a pale yellow cactus. We tiptoed past him on our way to the kitchen, where we'd stuff our backpacks with juice boxes and junk food and sneak out the back door.

Without Mama, we Dunegan kids did as we pleased. We rode our bikes right through downtown Brunswick in the afternoon sun. We never wore the hats and sunscreen Mama insisted upon, but dared the hot Georgia sun to fry our brains and blister our skin. We played Crazy Eights for money, watched TV well past midnight, and ate whatever we wanted.

Sometimes, if he was having a good day, Daddy took us to Connor's on Old Jesup Road. There we ordered meatloaf, honey glazed ham, chicken fried steak. Banana cream pie. Chocolate brownie sundae. When Mama was gone, we were obsessed with food.

"How you doin', Foster?" The folks at Connor's loved our Daddy.

"Doin' fine," Daddy always answered. "How 'bout you?"

Some of the men asked after Mama. "Your old woman leave you again?"

"She shore did." Daddy answered with a smile. We all knew they were joking.

After a couple of beers, Daddy introduced us again and again to the folks who were seated in the bar. They were polite enough to act like we were new items. "Damn fine kids," Daddy always said of us. "This here's my boy." Daddy put his arm across Adrian's shoulders. "And these are my girls." He waved his cigarette. "Michaelena is gonna be a heartbreaker, and Christina is gonna to have her heart broken."

Christina and I never got used to those introductions. We understood they had to do with men and women and love and suffering, the worst part of a fairy tale, but we were not sure how those warning labels matched up to us. I looked like my Daddy, blue-eyed and skinny with muddy yellow hair, but he was the one nursing his heart when Mama took off. Christina looked like Mama, soft and round with freckles like droplets of buckwheat honey, but she was dreamy and cried when her feelings were hurt. Was Daddy saying that Christina was like him and I was like Mama?

Whenever Daddy made those introductions, I imagined myself Wonder Woman stomping on red, valentine-shaped hearts while Christina pictured her heart lying crushed behind her ribs in a pile of red glass shards. We were determined never to fall in love.

The summer I was fourteen, Adrian thirteen, and Christina twelve, Mama found herself mixed up with a full-fledged spiritual commune called Contentment. "Would you believe it?" Mama was beside herself. "I met them in Darien, but they have a farm in Ohio, directly across the river from West Virginia."

Adrian, who was more geographically-minded than you might think, did some quick calculation. "Yankees," he said in a spiteful voice.

According to Mama, members of Contentment did more than concentrate on prayer and good works. They raised poinsettias and Easter lilies; they made pine wreaths, potpourri, and scented candles; they carved eagles, hand-stitched red, white, and blue quilts, and stenciled the rebel and union flags on all manner of things. They unloaded their wares at craft shows and reenactment fairs and through mail order catalogs. Having tax-exempt church status also helped.

"God led me to them," Mama explained when she signed on to spend six weeks riding around Civil War sites as a cook in Contentment's latest venture, a portable barbecue stand. We could imagine Mama ladling barbecue onto sesame seed buns and thanking customers with a joyful "God bless you," but we had trouble featuring her inside a cook wagon that was nothing more than a tiny mobile home. Mama despised mobile homes, and her greatest fear was weather. Maybe she was safe from hurricanes there in the middle of Pennsylvania or Virginia or Maryland, but we knew tornadoes touched down everywhere. "I'm in good hands," she always said when she called from Gettysburg or Chancellorsville or Antietam. "Don't you fret."

"No, ma'am," we said.

In those days of Mama being gone and Daddy being left behind, we contemplated the discrepancies of love. How could love both hold us together and pull us apart? How could it make Daddy so miserable and Mama so flighty? Why, we wondered, would Mama consider Daddy an answer to her prayers? Or, better yet, what exactly was she praying for? By the time Daddy found Mama hitchhiking along Route 6, he was past forty and already sickly. He had bad lungs from smoking cigarettes and working in the sawmill and bad knees from his days in the Army. He had spent all his money on Lucille and was in no market for another woman.

"Someday you'll find out yourselves," Daddy told us. "You got no power over who you fall in love with. Love hits you like a Mack truck and leaves you flattened and senseless."

I never quite believed Daddy, mainly because I was convinced no man would dare to run me down with his love. But in our Daddy's case, I might could imagine Mama flattening him like an eighteen-wheeler. There he was a grown man from a faraway state, a man likely wishing he was young and free again, when a bold Yankee girl suddenly climbed into his truck and promised she would stick to him forever. Mama was like sunlight though a heavy coastal fog, Daddy said. What normal man could turn away from all that brightness?

One day I came home from my friend Muriel's to discover a darling convertible parked in front of our duplex. In the backyard, I found two strange boys. Older, cute, blond boys, who were taller than Daddy and not dressed like the Mormon missionaries he usually put up with. These guys stood over Daddy's tomato vines with polite smiles on their tanned faces while Daddy pointed out the biggest Big Boy in his patch. Maybe they were college boys, summer interns from the County Agricultural office.

Adrian stood at the far end of the garden, tossing his penknife at the wooden stakes and showing off. Christina sat on the porch steps looking flushed and hopeful, as opposed to the flushed, worried look she wore when the Mormons came around. As for Daddy, he was shining like a circus spotlight. His beam landed on me. "Michaelena, come right this way. I got me two fellows I want you to meet."

The cute boys turned toward me, and immediately I felt wrinkled and sticky and uncommonly shy. "Michaelena is my oldest girl." Daddy said. I waited for him to go on about me being a heartbreaker, but the boys were offering me their broad, long-fingered hands.

"Nate," said the one wearing khaki shorts.

"Douglas," said the one in cutoffs.

Their hands were smooth and warm, and I hoped with all my might that my own hand would not feel like a damp kitchen sponge.

They asked me the standard questions that folks always asked of *children*: what grade was I in, how was my summer, was I ready for school to start, blah, blah, blah. I tried not to take offense and considered asking them if they had girlfriends and how they might feel about taking me and Muriel out for a long drive in their sweet little car.

"Good to see you, sir." They shook Daddy's hand. "Good to know you," they called as they drove down Richmond Street with their blond heads aglow.

"Who were those masked men, Pop?" Adrian tried out his best cowboy voice.

"They belong to an old lady friend of mine." Daddy matched Adrian's tone, and we could tell he was having a good day.

"Someone you knew before Mama?" Christina reclaimed Daddy by standing right at his side and hooking her finger through his belt loop.

"Someone I knew long before your mother."

Nate and Douglas came to visit us off and on during that summer Mama was in the barbeque wagon. They brought us sparklers and ice cream bars and water pistols. They teased me and Christina until we blushed like we'd been scalded. We decided we wanted to marry them someday. Yessir, these were boys to take a chance on.

Go ahead, Love, run us over.

We never questioned why those gorgeous boys came around to see Daddy and his attention-starved children on a regular basis. Maybe we didn't want to acknowledge they were all there was to Daddy's dreaded Other Family. Maybe if we spoke, they might vanish again.

On his good days, Daddy stayed outside, shirtless and whistling as he fussed with his garden. On his bad days, he was in his recliner with his cigarettes and Old Crow on the TV tray beside him. But even then, when he smelled like Ben Gay and whiskey, we recognized that Daddy was our constant. Our Mama may wander some, but unlike Lucille, she wouldn't take us away. We would never lose track of *our* Daddy.

That summer, unlike any other summer, we anticipated Mama's return. We knew she would be in her glory, full of high spirits and improbable stories of good works, swooping through the house to dispense hugs and kisses and call us her *babies*. Love and marriage and husbands and wives might be unpredictable, easy about slipping through our hands, but thanks to Nate and Douglas, we had proof that blood bound us together.

Go ahead, Love, take us on. We Dunegans are mighty, as tough and pliant as the twining green runners of Daddy's summer squash.

Vernal Equinox

Frank didn't let Margaret take the car as much as he used to. He blamed it on the weather. "March in Northwestern Pennsylvania is too unpredictable," he told her. "You best stay home."

In fact, his decision was due to Margaret's recent tendency to drive off and then forget where she was going. She'd leave to get milk or bread at Evanberry's Golden Dawn and come home empty-handed. One time last week she had gone over the state line into Ohio. "The road just kept going," she said, raising her hands in good humor.

Frank was afraid that someday she might forget to come back. Not because her memory was faulty, he had no worry of that. It was more like she was paying attention to something he could not see or hear.

Reading the morning paper while eating his eggs and toast, Frank noticed that the Crisis Hot Line was looking for volunteers. He knew Margaret was quite capable of working with people, and he expected she might also be good in a crisis, especially one that befell someone else. He glanced up from his paper, casting around in his mind for a way to mention the article on page three.

Margaret, dreamily packing his lunch at the kitchen counter, sensed his attention. "I once had a rich man love me," she said as she spread mayonnaise on whole wheat.

Surely he heard wrong. "What's this now?"

"I was eighteen." Margaret held the mayonnaise knife in mid-air. "I was eighteen, fresh out of high school, and working as a salad girl at the Yacht Club."

He put his newspaper down and waited for the punchline. Margaret looked perfectly normal there in her blue wool bathrobe and furry slippers. Yes, her figure had rounded out some over the years, but Frank preferred flesh to bone.

"Michael Gleason was very extravagant, you know." The overhead light caught a glint of gray in her tousled brown hair. "He gave me diamonds in everything. A bracelet inside a can of tennis balls." She held her index finger and thumb close together. "Narrow and shiny as Christmas tree tinsel. Another time he gave me a ring, covered with chocolate and placed in a gold foil box."

"Covered in chocolate," Frank repeated. "What did you do with it?"

"My mother made me give it back at the end of the summer." She zipped sandwiches into plastic bags and filled Frank's thermos. "Before he left for college, Michael gave me another diamond. An unset stone nestled into the petals of a red rose. Like a teardrop." She turned to Frank, the steaming silver thermos held between them. "I kept that diamond and didn't tell my mother. Then I lost it."

"How could you lose a diamond, Margaret?"

"It fell out of the tissue paper and into the floor register in my bedroom. Into the furnace, I guess." Her forehead pulled in thought. "What would I have done with it anyway?"

~~~

There were a few sudden warm days in early March, a sweet tease before another record-breaking snowfall passed over them, and Margaret grew glum. Somehow, without even trying, she had become one of those women who were always cold. Always. Despite wearing gloves and wool socks long into spring, sometimes, even deep into summer, she felt a chill climb her spine and lick across her neck like a cold tongue. Over the long winter the forced-air furnace dried her skin, gave her nosebleeds, and made her eyes scratchy no matter how many times she refilled the tea-kettle on the stove. She sat in the bathtub, sunk to her neck in hot water, and thought about those years she had never been cold. Those years when she had been younger and chasing after children, carpooling to one activity after another, wearing shorts and skimpy shirts from May to October. She had been slender and supple-skinned and impervious to the change of seasons or the drop of temperatures.

"What am I going to do when we're old, Frank?" She added another blanket to their bed. "I know old people are always cold, but how much colder could I be?"

Frank, comfortable in pajama bottoms and T-shirt, lay with his hands folded behind his head, his narrow nose pointed toward the ceiling. He spoke with his eyes closed. "Some subfreezing morning we'll get into the car and drive south until we feel warm. Then we'll stop and spend the winter." At night, his voice was deep and slow, the voice that Margaret associated with reading bedtime stories to their children or helping them with homework. She almost expected him to recite, *And then the little Red Hen said* . . . or to talk about solving for x.

Margaret turned off the lamp and fit herself to his lean frame, her head in the hollow between his shoulder and ribcage. She rubbed her socked feet against Frank's bare soles. "How long do we have to wait to drive south?"

"Not long. Until I retire."

Margaret added up time and sighed. They were barely sixty, and Frank, she knew, would probably stay on as long as the meat processing plant let him. Even on his days off, Frank was not one to be idle. He had already ordered seeds and plotted next summer's vegetable garden on graph paper.

She yawned as Frank's warmth wrapped around her. He shifted his arms, turned his body, and they curled toward sleep, spine to spine, as they had virtually every night for thirty-eight years. They had been separated only by three childbirths and the occasional visiting relatives who took up more space than Margaret and Frank had to comfortably offer. Only death or disease would separate them now, Margaret figured. She imagined their spines gradually fusing together, like conjoined twins, until they would no longer be able to move apart, even briefly.

Winter would be bearable, Margaret decided, if she could only go to bed until spring finally came. Well, why not? Like the groundhog that popped out of the ground every February and then thought better of it, she, too, would stay in her bed until the weather changed.

First, however, she baked. Chicken and meatloaf and vegetable lasagna. Brownies and apple turnovers and pies from last summer's frozen fruit. She arranged dinners on Styrofoam plates, slipped them into food storage bags, and stacked them in the freezer. Twelve plates. Twelve dinners for Frank.

Next Margaret walked to the new shop on Water Street where she took her time inhaling fragrant cheeses and coffee blends. She selected boxes of tea and anise cakes, a tin of Walker's Shortbread and small jars of imported jelly. She bought bottles of exotic fruit juice and Perrier, a variety of hard rolls for her brie, gouda, and edam, a few bars of dark, dark chocolate.

At the library, she checked out an armload of romances, mysteries, three biographies of presidents' wives, and an anthology of women's poetry. "Do you happen to know," Margaret asked a librarian, "which woman author it was that wrote her poetry in bed? Under an umbrella?"

"Any number of them, I imagine."

At home Margaret stacked her boxes and bottles under the bed and arranged the cheese and rolls on the north-facing windowsill. To prevent spoilage. She stacked her books alongside the food items and searched the linen closet for the package of pretty sheets she had been saving for a special occasion. She sang "Respect" as she made the bed and thought of their oldest daughter. Retha was named for Aretha Franklin, but only Margaret knew that. Frank thought it was a family name.

She covered the sheets and two blankets with her grandmother's quilt. Sleeping under those deep majestic colors and star-like stitches was certain to order her thoughts and re-shape her life. Yes indeed, Margaret was ready to wait out winter in style and comfort, and she felt better than she had in months.

~~~

By Sunday, the third day of Margaret's protest against Winter, Frank was no longer amused. "Whatever makes you feel better," he had said at first, not considering the possibility of her whim lasting longer than a day or two. Oh, he had gone about his chores yesterday, planting onion sets and peas in spite of the bitter wind, but today he felt at loose ends. Displaced. The house was too quiet and suddenly very large without Margaret following him around to tell him what she had heard from the kids or seen on television or read in one of the books she was always carrying under her arm. He walked from room to room turning on lights, the radio, the television. He looked around the quiet order of the house and tried hard to find something out of place, something missing.

Sunday was Margaret's favorite day, the day when she slept late, made a large breakfast and no lunch, and went off to church. As regular as clockwork. Now here it was time for Sunday services and Margaret was still in bed, reading about Abigail Adams and watching Charles Osgood on television. He poured himself a cup of coffee and went to have a talk with her.

"How nice of you to bring me coffee," she said when he came into the room.

He handed her his mug as if that had been his intention all along and watched her take a cautious sip. Propped against soft blue-green pillows, she looked very young. Her eyes were a lighter green than usual and her face was pink and unlined. "You comfortable?" he asked, for something to say. He could tell she was comfortable, content as a child home on a snow day from school.

"Very cozy. Want to join me?" Margaret playfully pulled back the bed covers.

Frank knew in less than two minutes he could take off his clothes and slide between those warmed sheets and have her soft flesh pressed against the sharpness of his bones. He could be content too. But his unwillingness to give in or maybe her recent talk of diamonds and Michael Gleason held him back.

"Tell me about your garden." She appeared unaware he had rejected her offer.

"It was muck. I took a chance on the peas. The onions will make it."

She nodded over the coffee cup and patted the bed for him to sit down. He ignored that gesture, too.

"When I can work the ground, I'll put in the carrots and radishes. Then maybe I'll try turnips and beets."

"It will be lovely. You have such a green thumb, Frank."

"So you're staying here?"

Margaret stretched contentedly. "Before you came up I dreamed I was driving in a city, can you imagine that? Just zooming along these narrow overpasses and bridge ramps of someplace like Pittsburgh or Cleveland or Washington, D.C., cities where I'd never in my real life ever drive. In this dream, I came off a twisting ramp, and there before me was an endless smoky valley of identical houses, two-story dirty brick houses, like a mill town."

"Not many mill towns left nowadays."

"It was breathtaking, Frank. Like I had arrived in a foreign land under my very own power."

"What does that mean, Margaret?"

"I really don't know." She smiled and waved as he went out the door. "Come back again," she said. Like a salesclerk dismissing a customer.

Then came three sunny days, days that promised blossoms and new green leaves. Frank went up to the bedroom when he heard Margaret singing "Stop in the Name of Love," and there she was, still in her night-gown and remaking the bed. He stopped in the doorway to watch the quick, smoothing movement of her hands.

She smiled. "Hey there, you."

"Hey yourself. What's new?"

"Cousin Nancy called and I told her we would have Easter here." She shook the pillows into their cases, fluffing and forming them.

"Easter is in two weeks, Margaret. It could still snow. You know that."

"The light will be stronger then." She hugged a pillow to her. "I will be able to feel the difference between dawn and dusk. The earth will thaw. The air will be softer. Soft enough to smell. You know all about this, Frank," she said. "You know the minute spring comes."

~~~

Wind rattled the windows, snow bounced against the glass like icy pebbles, and Frank and Margaret made love for the first time since she'd taken to her bed. She could feel him coming back to her, forgiving her for her odd behavior. The warmth moved between them, through them, back and forth like the motion of a river in July. Warm. She was warm.

Frank fell deep into sleep with the light on. From relief, no doubt, that his life had been restored. Margaret understood his need to have things stay the same, his inability to follow her to a different place. She considered creeping down the steps and through the cold house to her desk, the dainty secretary she had brought to her marriage filled with childhood books, old letters, and report cards. She imagined pulling out the small vertical tray shaped like a pillar and unwrapping the tissue pa-per, watching for the sparkle, the glitter of Michael's last gift, in the dim light from the window.

She turned out the light and curved her spine against Frank's. She did not need to leave their warm nest to verify the existence of her ear-lier life. Michael Gleason, who had chosen Margaret from among all those young, pretty girls working at the Yacht Club, had been no more than a pleasant flirtation, a quick, welcome glimpse into a future that promised life beyond salad-making. Someday one of Margaret's children would find

Michael's diamond and wonder over it. But for now, spring was coming. Soon her life would change again. Things would happen she had never considered. She closed her eyes and tried to estimate how far she could drive into her dreams and still return to Frank by morning.

Decoration Day

As a child, Lyda was assured that pride goeth before a fall. Now, these many decades later, it is clear she is finally falling in a headlong, angry descent. Her modest pride in being the oldest, the wisest, the only remaining member of the Tomlinson family has been washed away by the responsibility of tending to the many earthly possessions of those other departed souls. Lyda finds it impossible to part with anything, not Mama's Haviland nor Uncle Elvery's Masonic cufflinks, not Grandfather's board and batten house nor Alice's gilt-edge, broken-spined confirmation Bible.

Rock bottom rises to meet her when she realizes she alone must also tend to the graves. For every spring-green May since childhood, Lyda has had her sister Alice, so strong and agreeable, to share the task. Alice would dig and Lyda would plant; Alice would water and Lyda would weed. But this year, for no good reason that Lyda can discover, Alice has died. Gone off and left her, as if out of spite.

At the last of the cemeteries, next to the split rail fence, Lyda parks Uncle Elvery's old Chevy. She notices the car's black exterior is grayed by a permanent film of dust and bat droppings as she contemplates how many trips she will have to make between the car, Uncle Elvery's grave, and the water spigot. Here everything hangs on the side of a hill.

Fair Meadows Cemetery, perched on the eastern edge of Ohio, is home to more creatures than Lyda has seen in a year's time. A red-winged blackbird takes flight as she braces herself against the car, and a ground-hog dashes across the field beyond the fence row. A green haze hangs in the air, reflecting the radiance of freshly mown hillside. It is just shy of noon, and the sun burns sticky and hot. Lyda removes her cardigan and adjusts her straw hat to her hairdo, re-silvered and permed the day before she flew out of Clearwater.

She decides to carry the flat of flowers first and come back for the watering can and the peat moss, the spade and the trowel. The plastic tray with one red geranium and a half dozen white and purple petunias weighs next to nothing, but it is cumbersome, and Lyda cannot see over it. Her feet and the ground beneath them are hidden from view.

Lyda has walked with caution all her life—well before Uncle Elvery's fatal fall in the cow pasture. *Exposure* was recorded on his death certificate, but Lyda has her doubts. The cows had been sold off decades before Elvery's calamity, and for him to be anywhere on the lower side of the barn was extremely unlikely.

Lyda knows she has good reason to be suspicious of sudden death.

The lay of the land at Fair Meadows appears to have changed since last year, becoming steeper and less well-tended than she remembered. The tree with the umbrella shaped top, their guidepost in locating Elvery's grave, is missing, and she will have to wander up and down each row of tombstones to find their plot. Of course, Alice—had she been here—would have had no trouble. Even with the change in terrain from the 1985 tornadoes, Alice had instinctively gone directly to the right spot. She had a keen sense of direction and always knew which way to turn in traffic. There was simply no reason for her to have pulled onto that bypass in the wrong lane.

Lyda's route through squat granite slabs and slender marble markers feels misdirected. These rows are too narrow, the grave sites look too new, too small. The names inscribed on stone are too foreign-sounding. Her arms are beginning to ache, and if she were not so angry, she would sit down here among the Kolcheskys and weep. Alice should have realized this would be the result of leaving her alone. Her death is nothing less, Lyda decides, than a selfish lack of consideration.

Of course it was Alice's idea to buy this plot of graves in such a god-forsaken corner of the county. "We can see the farm from here," Alice had said, gleefully pointing to a spot on the horizon. "Look, right there, just above the water tower and a little to the left."

Lyda squints across the horizon now. The haze has lifted considerably, but she cannot make out anything recognizable. She has, in fact, never been able to find any of the landmarks Alice so eagerly claimed to see. Lyda knows buying the cemetery plots had less to do with the view and more to do with the salesman who came around to the farm on a regular basis during the war. He was heart-quickening handsome, Alice and Lyda decided the first time they saw him. He wore a suit and a Panama hat. "From Florida," he said, twirling the hat over his fingers. "Where the sunshine is clear and strong and quick to dry up the slightest hint of rain."

It was threatening rain as he spoke, and Lyda was about to question the wisdom of wearing his prize hat into uncertain weather when Alice exclaimed her pleasure at having "such an extensive traveler come to call," and welcomed him into the parlor and gave him her freshly-squeezed lemonade. "Also from Florida," she said, referring to the lemons.

"You ladies have been there?" He smiled a perfect, white smile in a tanned, movie star face. His hair was as black as a crow's feather and swept neatly away from his widow's peak like the crest of a wave.

"Oh, we've never set foot out of Ohio, have we, Lyda?" Alice wore her favorite apron, the blue dotted Swiss with ruffles around the bib, and her face was rosy and her eyes bright. As pretty and poised, Lyda noticed, as she would have been in her Sunday silk blouse.

"Pittsburgh," Lyda said. "We went by train to Pittsburgh with Mama once."

"I don't remember," Alice said. "We must have been children." Alice gave Lyda a look as if to say she wished her silent. Or gone.

"Train travel is a great way to see the country," the salesman said, shining his smile directly on Lyda this time. "You could catch a train in Cleveland and be in Tampa in no time at all."

"We have a lot of work to keep us here, Mr. Bailey," Lyda said, reading the nameplate on his briefcase. "The garden, the chickens." She waved toward the window and the empty barn beyond.

"Call me Matthew." He extended his hand to envelop her fingers in a dry, warm grasp. "I'm a local boy. From Andover." He held on to her hand as he talked. "Came home to enlist, but turns out I have a weak back." He winked at Alice. "I'm gonna work on strengthening it so Uncle Sam will take me later. Employment with Fair Meadows is strictly temporary."

Alice raised the hem of her apron to her mouth, touched by his patriotism. Lyda gently withdrew her hand from Matthew's and cupped his warmth into her palm.

Lyda cannot find the cemetery caretaker's house and wonders if it has burned down to the ground during her winter in Florida. To her left and farther down the hill, there is a very tall stand of familiar evergreens, and Lyda walks toward them. Along the way, she leaves the tray of plants with the Beckingers. Their showy monument, four carved sides of tall gray granite with an angel at its crown, stands in direct line between a flowering dogwood and the fence row. Surely, Lyda thinks, she can find her plants again, once she has located the graves.

Lyda stands beside Samuel Beckinger's VFW marker to shade her eyes with her long, narrow hand. Her back and shoulders ache from the plantings she did last evening at Mama and Papa's graves, which are right in town on a flat lot, not cattywompus against a hillside. Lyda can just make out a pitch of rooftop under some trees which must be the care-taker's. She plans her route: straight across the rim of shrubbery and then downhill, hopefully on a path.

Matthew Bailey talked about traveling every time he came around, always carrying his Panama hat in one hand and his personalized brief-case in the other. "The sand at St. Petersburg Beach is as fine and white as salt," he told them, "and the water in the Gulf is azure, as clear and blue as Alice's eyes."

Alice had smiled at that remark, while Lyda tried to recall when, if ever, she had heard the word *azure* spoken right out loud.

"It's great for swimming," he said to Lyda. "Warm as bath water." There was an intimacy in the way Matthew Bailey spoke that made the blood gather at the base of her neck and spread across her throat and up-ward to her cheeks. It wasn't his words precisely, but the way his eyes moved, studying her mouth when he said *warm* and returning her gaze on *bath water*.

Across the table, Lyda saw the same warm flush reflected on Alice's face. "You swim?" Alice asked in a quivery, timid voice.

"Everyone does." Matthew pushed his arms onto the table top, forc-ing Mama's best tablecloth into ripples of lace. Fine, black hairs curled from under his starched white cuff. "At the far end of the beach there is a great, pink hotel, the size of a palace, where famous people stay," Matthew told them. "You can walk down there and swim in the same water with them."

"Movie stars?" Alice, too, leaned forward, her elbows pushing the lace cloth in from her side of the table.

"Movie stars." Matthew nodded solemnly, his forehead slightly creased under the dip of his dark hair. "Zelda and Scott Fitzgerald used to stay there."

"Imagine that," Alice said with a sense of awe.

"There's a lot of great people in Florida. Presidents and royalty. Artists and such. Hemingway and Dickinson lived there, too."

Lyda was about to question who Dickinson might be, but Alice jumped to her feet, insisting he must have a piece of fresh apple cake.

He told them he had given up his traveling job as sales representative for a castings company in Baltimore to come home and enlist, and now that he was here, he just might stay. "Even if I can get Uncle Sam to take me," he said, waving his fork, "a soldier needs a place to come home to."

The caretaker's house has been freshly painted. Set under a clump of poplars where the lane dips over the hillside, it seems too white to be real. Lyda has to shade her eyes again to look in its direction, but at least the ground is fairly even here, and the walking easier. Her denim blue Keds pick up the pace, matching an old refrain that runs through her head: *Matthew Bailey will come back, come back, come back. Matthew Bailey will come back.*

Alice and Lyda assured themselves daily of Matthew's return once he was finally allowed to enlist. Weak back or not, he was needed, and he left at once. "I expect you ladies to write." He was cheerful, trying to ignore Alice's tears and shuddering sighs as she served him her gingerbread with lemon sauce. "Send me the local news."

"Of course we will," Lyda told him, astonished to hear her own voice crack and dissolve into a hoarseness that hung on for days after Matthew departed. "Fact is, Alice and I are considering going to work at Ohio Rubber until all you boys come back."

"Won't be much longer now, I'd say." He set his pink glass cake plate carefully on the table and stood with a solemn sense of ceremony, his hands in his jacket pockets, his eyes lowered. "I appreciate your kindness all these months, and I want you to know I won't forget it." He looked at them then, one at a time, for a good long minute, and then held out his hand.

"Before you go," Lyda said, her voice starting to break again, "Alice and I wish to buy a plot in Fair Meadows."

They purchased eight gravesides. Eight. A foolish, outrageous purchase for two maiden ladies, each one on either side of thirty with no prospect of husbands or children in sight. It had, at the time, been the most patriotic gesture Lyda could think to make. Now, forty years later, it is an embarrassment to her.

"Eight? You have an plot of eight?" the caretaker's wife asks Lyda. "What are the names on the markers?"

"One marker," Lyda says. "Elvery Tomlinson." She spells both first and last names for the young woman, who is bent over a book of plot plans. They are in the front room of the caretaker's house. A small room with too much furniture and too many family photographs on the walls, it smells like it has been shut up under these trees too long. The windows faced away from the splendid view of hills and valleys as well as the neighborhood reminders of mortality.

The young woman traces one finger along each name in her book while her other hand holds her pale hair back from her face. She is flushed from the effort to help, and Lyda becomes exhausted watching her. She is considering sinking into the upholstered chair next to the desk when the girl looks up.

"There's only one person buried there?"

Lyda nods.

"What about the owner's name?"

"The same: Tomlinson. Either Alice or Lyda Tomlinson. Maybe both."

"Here it is." The girl turns, her finger marking a place on the page.

"Tomlinson, A. and E. It's on the other side of the drive where you came in."

The other side of the drive. Lyda knows, without looking in the direction indicated by the girl's outstretched hand, where to go. She has turned in the wrong direction. It is a lifelong habit, the one fault Alice found to tease her about, and the reason Alice always drove. Lyda feels better as she retraces her steps from the caretaker's place back to her plants. It is uphill, but not unpleasant. Lyda imagines she can hear Alice chiding her. *For someone so smart, Lyda Jane Tomlinson, you never learned right from left.*

The sun is strong and bright and reflects off the markers and the pebbles in the path. It catches the white stripes in the veterans' flags and sends dazzling light into Lyda's eyes. The heat and the clean-smelling air at the top of the hill remind Lyda of the beach at St. Petersburg that first summer she and Alice went to Florida.

82

Alice had taken off her sandals and pulled her skirt to her knees to walk across the white sand and wade into the Gulf. "It *is* like bath water," she called to Lyda, "just like Matthew told us."

They found the big, pink hotel, closed and in disrepair, and stayed in a tourist home a few blocks beyond it. They walked the beach in the mornings and napped in the heat of the afternoons. And every evening, they dressed in their soft summer dresses and chose a different restaurant set at the water's edge. They told each other they liked to watch the people, to determine which ones were tourists like themselves, and which ones were natives. They liked to watch the women flirt and listen to the men talk about deep sea fishing or financial investments.

It was not until the night they decided to try drinking Orange Blossoms (they liked the name, and they liked orange juice, and the waiter had recommended them as a specialty of the house), as the house band played "Don't Fence Me In," that they admitted they were looking for Matthew Bailey. That they hoped he might return to one of his old haunts on the very night they were dining there.

"He wouldn't even know us, would he, Lyda?" Alice folded her hands around the stem of her glass and leaned forward. Her face was pink and freckled from the sun. "He would never be able to imagine us off the farm."

"We do look a bit more citified now," Lyda said, running her fingers through her wavy, newly-bobbed hair.

"We are becoming experienced travelers." Alice waved her empty glass at their waiter. "We are not as . . . as . . . what's the word I want, Lyda?"

"Backward?"

"We are not as backward." Alice nodded vigorously, her chin tapping the lace collar of her dress. "Is that why he didn't come back, do you think? Were we too backward?"

"It's possible he was killed in action," Lyda said, although they both knew otherwise. His name was never listed among those killed or missing.

Lyda retrieves the flat of plants from the Beckinger plot and returns to the car that had been Uncle Elvery's last. She knows it is ancient and unsightly, but it serves her purposes during these brief spring visits. Maybe, now that Alice is gone and the tenants have moved out without paying their rent, Lyda *will* sell Grandfather's farm. It will be a test of her ability to survive without the rest of them, to be decisive when she has to be.

Maybe she *will* auction the land, the crumbling barn, the house and its few remaining contents, the car, all of it in one fell swoop. Alice, after all, was truly the sentimental one.

The car starts with little coaxing, and Lyda carefully maneuvers between the fence and a marble obelisk to retrace her route back to the gate and proceed to the other side of Fair Meadows. She parks under the oak that has always been here and sights the umbrella shaped tree that will lead her down the path to Uncle Elvery's resting place. The ground feels familiar underfoot and her line of vision rests on the horizon. She imagines Uncle Elvery in his Sunday white shirt and dark suspenders shuffling in the distance, right where the sunlight reflects off the pale columns of birch.

The one lone tombstone on its green island of grass is plain and simple, as Elvery would have wanted. Lyda kneels slowly, fighting the stiffness in her knees, and dusts a family of spiders from their nest in the last digit of Elvery's death date, 1960. Twelve years before that, in 1948, Alice and Lyda had moved to Clearwater. The war was long over and it was fairly certain Matthew Bailey was not returning to Ohio. They convinced Uncle Elvery to leave Andover and keep the farm for them, to give them a chance to sample life in Florida.

Those first twelve years in Florida seemed like no time at all. They worked as secretaries for an insurance company, they bought a very small house with the rest of the money Mama left them, and every day was sunny and warm and very full of friends and parties and suppers along the beach. It was, Lyda thought, as if all those days in Florida had been a tourist promotion for one long day at the beach.

"We shouldn't have left him, Lyda," Alice had said at Elvery's funeral service. "We should have come home to check on him more often."

"He was happy alone," Lyda told her. "When we suggested he leave that rented room on Plum Street and come keep the farm for us, he thought he'd already died and gone to heaven."

"Lyda." Alice gasped at Lyda's irreverence, but the few mourners were out of earshot, gathered by the fake water fountain in the lobby to compare property taxes.

"It's true." Lyda reached out to shake Martha McKendry's hand, and Alice never mentioned it again.

The hot sun strikes Lyda's back in the same intense way it had when she tended Alice's grave, and she wonders—as she has for weeks—

whether the grave site in Clearwater was the cemetery Alice would have wanted. Would she have preferred to come to Fair Meadows and spend eternity alone with Uncle Elvery? Lyda thinks not.

Death was nothing they had discussed, and it had taken Lyda a couple of days to decide that she herself would prefer the old viney cemetery on the edge of the Clearwater and that Alice would simply have to be happy with her decision. Of course, Alice was easily satisfied. She would have probably been content with that modern place in the suburbs where there were no monuments, no flowers, nothing but a wrought iron fence to signify to passersby that it was more than an empty field.

Lyda stands to spade up the grassy earth and again feels the soreness in her shoulders. She holds tightly to the handle and steps firmly down on the top of the blade. She senses the tear of grass as she steps again and again, forming a small circle in the sod.

Lyda wonders if Alice has any idea how much effort it took to find two grave sites right in the heart of the old Clearwater cemetery. How she spent hours tracking down heirs to one of the few empty plots in the place, haggling over a price, and paying far more than she should have simply for the atmosphere that came from huge, mossy oaks and old weathered stones and brilliant flowering shrubs. As if that would make Alice eternally happy.

Lyda has already decided that happiness is beyond her own reach. Even when she is in the midst of doing something she likes and having a fine time, Lyda never feels quite content. After they retired, she and Alice took up oil painting, carting their easels and canvases along the waterfront. Alice had a fondness for birds and plant life, while Lyda preferred the inanimate docks and bait shops for her subjects. They both loved playing cards with their women friends and dancing at the Senior Center where widowers were plentiful, but Lyda always had a sense of being incomplete, of missing out on something she couldn't give a name to. Even in all those years of speculating about Matthew Bailey and how their lives might have been different upon his return, Lyda knew it wouldn't have mattered.

"You would have married him, stayed in Ohio, and I would have come to Florida alone," Lyda told Alice on more than one occasion.

"But it was my idea to come to Florida," Alice said a few months ago, out of the blue, as she dusted the collection of sea glass and driftwood.

"I guess it was." Matthew may have planted the notion, but it was Alice who had breathed life into such an unlikely dream.

"I've always thought Matthew Bailey was the best thing to happen to us, Lyda. If it hadn't been for him, we'd still be in Ohio, in that cold and lonesome farmhouse." She held her feather duster under her chin, and glanced out the window at her birdbath. "I can't remember any more how it felt to want to marry him, can you?"

"Of course not."

Lyda sets the plants into the ground, adds peat moss to the loosened sod, and covers the delicate roots with care. She carries her watering can to the nearest spigot, thinking how easily tired she has become, how this chore takes twice the time and labor without Alice. The handle is rusted and hard to turn, but the water is there, cold and plentiful. She fills her can to a manageable weight and starts back, noticing how nice the flowers look, set off, as they are, from other gravesides.

Alice would approve, she thinks, and then, tired and weary, Lyda fights back tears as she remembers how very angry she is with Alice. Lyda has, after all, seen more than one talk show on after-death experiences. She knows perfectly well that Alice had the chance to come back, to move away from the white light and the heavenly music, to snap back to life there in the emergency room and finish out her time with Lyda. It is the only unkind act Alice has ever committed against her, but it is obviously irreversible.

Well, Lyda thinks as she waters Uncle Elvery's flowers, perhaps Alice's selfish departure makes up for Lyda's own guilty secret. As Alice in her heavenly realm probably now knows, she had remembered exactly what it was like to want Matthew Bailey. How she counted the days between his visits, unable to sleep because the moon was too bright or the night too alive with sound, how she walked through the dark rooms while Alice slept and anticipated his touch on her hands, the small of her back, her face after Alice left the room.

Lyda had been the one to walk him to his car while Alice tended the stove. Lyda heard his promises and shared his quick embraces, his darting kisses. It had been the one time in her life when Lyda expected things would change, when she carried the hope of something better and more exciting than she could imagine. When Matthew did not return after the war, Lyda thought for a while that she was to blame for expecting too much. But when Alice suggested Elvery come to the farm so they could go to Florida, Lyda understood it was the possibility of an adventure, a new, brave experience, that she truly longed for. Of course Alice had sensed Lyda's desire, had probably recognized it long before Matthew's departure.

You were right, Lyda tells Alice in her mind as she wipes her damp hands on her pant legs. If Matthew had come back after the war, we would not have gone to Florida. We would have become colder and lonelier waiting to be chosen and then questioning his choice. Once apart, we would have grown bitter, each refusing to give the other Papa's land or Grandfather's house or Mama's china and silver service. Our lives would have been without wonder.

Lyda pats the top of Elvery's stone, a farewell until next May, and arranges her planting equipment in the car's trunk. Letting go has suddenly become the easiest thing in the world, she decides as starts the engine, as easy as living can ever be. As she leaves Fair Meadows, its markers as sunlit as a white sand beach, Lyda imagines drinking lemonade with lots of ice, the way Alice always fixed it, and resting on the porch swing the last tenants have left in their rush to move on.

Fly

Kevin complains about flies when truly, I promise you, there are no flies to be seen. "Fly," he calls in the midst of his channel surfing, and I come in from the kitchen with the fly swatter that has become my appendage. I sit beside him on the couch, waiting and hopeful. I am ready to see flies. I am ready to stand and swing with the force of a tennis player. I am ready to kill and kill again with loud, satisfying thwacks.

Kevin has landed on MTV, and while the screen is busy and buzzing, there are no flies. "That's J. Lo," I say, "singing in Spanish."

"Sad," he says.

"Yes." I nod. It *is* sad, a mournful, lost love tune, but that doesn't keep J. Lo from simmering across the screen in a slow, sultry dance.

"Fly."

"Where?" I stand with swatter raised.

Kevin switches from MTV to FOX News. "Gone," he says, like he's given up hope I will ever save him from what only he can see.

After lunch, we walk to Pinewood Park. Kevin is a tall, lean man, a man who looks like he could run a mile and never be winded, and I am short and round with wide hips, muscled calves, and bad knees. Should Kevin decide to run, I wouldn't catch him.

We walk at least two miles a day, he sniffing the air like a hound and me dosed with arthritis medication. We are rounding the curve by the lake, when Kevin breaks his stride. "Fly, fly, fly."

I search the ground for dog droppings, for a bird carcass, or a discarded sandwich. Nothing. At this time of day, the park is quiet. Lunchtime joggers are back at work. Mothers with strollers are putting their babies down for naps. On the far side of the lake are three young women, college students, I'm guessing, trotting like colts. Kevin turns to watch them, his eyes as bright as the sky. Then, on the water, I see a shimmer of color, the wispy sensation of flight. "Kevin, did you see a dragonfly? Is that what you mean?"

"No." His eyes cloud. Then he starts off towards home, his longer stride perfectly transmitting his impatience with me. "No. Fly. Dragon."

"Is this normal?" I ask Kevin's doctor. "Are hallucinations typical for Early Onset patients?" I refuse to fully name anything with *early onset* so casually attached to it. Like Kevin is experiencing puberty. Or menopause.

"Well, Brenda." Dr. Bogue is slouching on his stool like a teenager, but now he leans towards me like we're old buddies at a neighborhood bar and launches into a long, rambling response. He throws in a few examples, an odd exception, and a couple of medical terms just to dazzle me. He believes he is charming. He believes that using my Christian name instead of *Mrs. Gorman* will prevent me from asking more questions.

"So seeing things is not unusual?" I am hoping he will argue with me, that he will say, *why, yes it is, Mrs. Gorman; perhaps your husband has been misdiagnosed.* I want him to tell me that Kevin has something they know how to fix.

"It's more common for our patients *not* to recognize what they see." He measures each word like he is doling out a great reward. "Rather than recognizing things that aren't there."

I say, "You don't really know, do you?" It's my best parting shot.

We are barely out the office door, when Kevin spins around to peer through the plate glass. "Fly," he says loudly.

"You saw a fly in Doctor Bogue's office?"

"No." He shakes his head, and Yvonne, the lovely receptionist, gives us a friendly wave.

On the way home, Kevin spots flies in front of the public library and across from the Dairy Queen. While we are stopped at the intersection of

Lincoln and Cherry, he points excitedly, claiming a fly on the windshield and later, one on the behind of a passing bicyclist. I wonder if I could be going blind.

We have cocktails with the Evening News. I need one by this time of the day, and I figure it can't hurt Kevin. Too late to worry about losing brain cells now. We sip martinis and watch one piece of bad news after another. The war in Iraq blazes on. Cheney is booed in Ohio, but Kerry and Edwards are gaining no ground in the polls or the hearts of Americans. Experts are expecting a shortage of flu vaccine.

Oh God, Superman has died.

I contemplate switching the channel. But wait. A young couple is arrested for having sex at the Alamo. "Cheers," I say, raising my glass.

"Fly," Kevin says, looking right into my eyes. "Fly time."

We did it everywhere when we were young. All the ordinary places and then some, beginning with our Icelandic Air flight to Amsterdam, where we had emergency row seats, good-sized blankets, and darkness working to our advantage. We were both thin then. It wasn't as tricky as you might imagine. Mostly we did it standing up and after dark. Up against a wall in the Waterloo Station and the far right column at the Jefferson Memorial. On the Metro and the Maid of the Mist. It helped that maxi-coats and granny dresses were in style then. Against a canyon wall in Death Valley and one of the great Sequoias. General Sherman, I believe it was. At a war protest and a George McGovern rally. It helped that we looked ordinary, more conservative than not.

"Hey, baby," Kevin would say, "let's fly," and we'd slip away. Into a doorway, between parked cars, or there on the grass between a boxwood hedge and a banner made of bedsheets and proclaiming "Eighteen Today, Dead Tomorrow."

I can't remember when we stopped. Or why, exactly. When you're married as long as we've been, you may have lots of opportunities to be creative, but things change. We had our daughter. I gained weight and lost my dexterity. Kevin took a job funded by taxpayers and lost his nerve. Our entire generation grew up and became stuffy.

Fly. Who would have guessed that I, the one claiming to have all her faculties, would be the one to forget? The one to so easily confuse a stellar verb with a commonplace noun? If Kevin and I had to live our lives all over again, I tell myself now, we would be more daring. We would cut classes and start at dawn, out on the dew-slippery quad. We would try out the

Coliseum, the Parthenon, the Great Pyramid, and Stonehenge. This time around, we would leave our daughter home with my mother or Kevin's father or a pierced, tattooed babysitter. We would travel to unconventional places, places accessible by ferry or donkey or zipline, carrying only what would fit on our backs.

The real disgrace, the real disaster, is never the one you can imagine. If we'd known that tidbit forty years ago, we would have made sex in public places an art form.

"Fly?" Kevin is watching me closely.

"Let's fly." I lead the way to the bedroom, so I don't have to see his disappointment and pretend I don't know that the last, strong, pulsing coil of Kevin's brain is set to the time when we were so demented by love the blood rushed from our brains and made us dizzy and aching and disdainful of beds. I shed my clothes as I go and pull Kevin down on top of me, a plump cushion for all his sharp angles and bony edges. "Soon," I lie as convincingly as I can. "Soon, baby, we'll fly as high and far as we can go."

Our daughter, Elizabeth, is planning a destination wedding. She is a beautiful girl who likes nice things, but when it comes to spending her own money, she has her father's common sense. Brant, her fiancé, does not. Their list of destination sites originally included a castle in Scotland, a beach on the Indian Ocean, and a villa in Venice, but Elizabeth vetoed them all in favor of something more domestic.

She comes to see us every other Sunday, during the time Brant's Chess Club meets, with a new list of possibilities. She has grown tentative around her father, I notice, like he is too distant or too fragile to hug, and there is that awkward extra beat of time between her "Hey, Daddy" and her embrace. Kevin, who lights up at the sound of her voice and holds her tight, his eyes closed to seal away the essence of her, must notice the change. Despite medical evidence to the contrary, I think it must break his heart.

"So, what do you have for us today?" I say brightly. I'm happy to notice she has chosen to sit beside her father on the sofa, but I suspect it's to avoid having to face him straight-on. Really, it's not until you're up close that you have the sense of a blank slate. Even from across the room, Kevin looks like a fit, rather attractive, older man.

"We've narrowed the old list." Elizabeth takes a notebook out of her leather bag. "And we've added a few new ones."

I hate the use of *we*. Mostly because I know Elizabeth is the one doing the research on wedding sites. Primarily because *we* inflates Brant into a larger-than-life version of his rather bland self. It's not that I don't like the guy; it's simply that Elizabeth deserves someone with a little more pizzazz. A take charge, I'll-do-that-for-you-honey kind of guy, who will put a little more oomph, and a little more of his own money, into these wedding plans. A guy more like her father.

"Right now, we're thinking someplace Western. We know Hawaii is too far, but there's a park overlooking the Golden Gate Bridge. There's also a lodge overlooking a waterfall in the Rocky Mountains."

"Would that be too cold?" The wedding is scheduled for late September.

"Well, there's a ranch in the Arizona desert that might be warmer."

"What about snakes?"

"Mom, why do you have to be so negative?" The notebook is closed and back in her bag. "Where do you want me to go? A beach in Florida like everyone else?"

"No, not all. September is hurricane season." I can't bring myself to tell her that my negativity is really her father's. In some bizarre husband-wife telepathy, all of Kevin's practical concerns are transferred to me and I dutifully give them voice.

To make amends, we leave Kevin to channel surf and go into the kitchen where I feed her carrot cake and spiced tea and ask safe questions about bridesmaids and flowers.

"It will be simple, Mom. Annalee holding wildflowers or maybe a single rose." Elizabeth is absorbed with smushing cake crumbs between her fork tines. "So, you think Daddy will be okay by September?"

"Okay in what way?"

"You know. Will he be able to manage a trip out West? Will he be able to fly?"

"Your father," I say with a perfectly straight face, "loves to fly."

"He won't change?"

Finally the bulb lights. Elizabeth is worried about how Kevin will look. She pictures him bent and drooling, rolling down the aisle or the beach or the mountain path in a wheelchair, and while I understand this might be a good time for a lecture on shallowness, on judging people by appearance, I also remember how I worried that my own father would act the fool at my wedding. "Your father will look great in a tux, honey. He could be a father-of-the-bride model."

wedding's almost a year away."

might be a tad more gray, but that's very distinguished, don't you

"Don't b.s. me, Mom."

"Your father," I begin, and then I weave together an epic that is part history, part romance, part adventure. Not bullshit, which is outright exaggeration, but more like voodoo. A spell I want to cast. I tell her Kevin is strong and athletic and likely to stay that way for a good many years. I tell her he is more docile than aggressive, not apt to rant and rave and shower her wedding guests with spittle. I tell her no matter what sort of wedding processional she has in mind, she can take hold of his arm with pride. "If worse comes to worst," I say. "I can prop him up right beside you."

That, too, is voodoo, because some days I feel too weak to carry on, but it doesn't matter now because Elizabeth is mopping at her eyes, which means I have said too much. "This is just so hard," she says. "So stressful."

"Well then, having your father at your wedding is one less thing for you to stress over," I say with calm assurance. "He'll be there." Another of my magical incantations. "In fact, I'm thinking maybe we'll take a few trips between now and the wedding, a few practice runs, so he'll be comfortable with traveling off to the destination of your choice." If I had pixie dust, I would sprinkle it now.

"Brant's and my choice." She corrects me.

"That's what I meant." Pure bullshit.

It turns cold early in November, but Kevin and I don't vary our routine. Routine is good, according to Dr. Bogue, the whiz kid. He also has dispensed a new drug he calls "promising." *Promising* has increased Kevin's appetite and added muscle to his wiry frame, so that he now looks like one of those men who go to the gym to prowl for a trophy wife. "Not so fast," I call when he darts ahead of me in the park. "You're turning into a damn jock."

Whether from the effects of the drug or because he has forgotten, Kevin no longer talks about flies, and I miss it. I rather liked his conviction that we could have sex wherever and whenever we wanted. Our present nighttime routine consists of cocktails, followed by dinner and television. Then, after Letterman's opening monologue, we sit for a few moments of silence before we heave ourselves off the sofa and get ready for bed. It's a tradition, really. In the old days, we had a nightcap and sat in the sunroom while Kevin went on about his job and I went on about Elizabeth's playgroup or her Brownie Troop or her AP classes. But once we wound down, we still had that moment of quiet, holding hands and staring out at the night. It makes it easier now, don't you see, to pretend we've already had our talking time and this silence is a mere continuation of our old pattern.

Tonight Kevin is agitated. He fidgets with the needlepoint pillows at our backs. He shuffles through insurance papers on the end table. He picks up Elizabeth's travel brochures from the coffee table and turns them over and over in his hands as if he is counting photos of waterfalls and rock formations and flowering cacti. *We could do this, Brenda,* he says, flapping the pages back and forth. *We're not so old that we couldn't travel, couldn't have a few more adventures.*

No, of course Kevin doesn't actually speak, but I hear his voice in my head, and I know these are his thoughts. Not thoughts as they must be now, all piecemeal and scattershot, but thoughts of the real Kevin speaking out from wherever it is his brain is being held captive these days. "I don't know about that, honey," I say. "I'm not as sturdy and quick on my feet as I used to be." I watch those faraway places flutter between his fingers and try to remember what I've read about the importance of sensory stimulation. In spite of all Dr. Bogue's blather about routine, wouldn't a change of scenery, the enticement of new sights, sounds, and smells activate the brain? Maybe tap into some little-used mental closet just waiting to store up new memories? "I'm not ruling it out," I say, "but let me think about it."

It rains solidly for the next ten days and we are stuck inside. So much for a daily routine. Kevin follows me around the house with the ever-present travel brochures and surprises me with an odd slice of memory at every turn. *Do you remember the woman we met on the train to Marseilles? The one with the see-through dress and no underwear?*

"I certainly do. A woman after your own heart."

More likely my wallet. Like the Gypsies in Rome.

"Honey, those kids were so little they could barely reach into your pocket."

It would be good for us to get away, Brenda. Soak up a little sun before winter settles in

"Where do you want to go, Kevin?"

This question usually slows him down, but his response time is improving.

Anywhere warm, babe. Anywhere with you.

Ah, always the charmer. "And how would we pay for this little vaca-tion, dear husband?"

Call Mike Button.

Mike Button is Kevin's financial advisor, the man I'm depending on to keep us out of the County Home for the Aged, so I can already guess his reaction to my request for frivolous funds.

"Maybe in the spring," I say.

You'll be busy with wedding plans by springtime.

Personally, I doubt that Elizabeth will share any more of her wedding plans with me, but we are seeing more of her now that Brant has advanced to the local Amateur Chess Finals.

"Brant doesn't want you to go and cheer him on?" I ask as I hang up her raincoat.

"He says I distract him."

That could be a compliment, but somehow I doubt it. "His loss is our gain," I say. "Come out to the sunroom for a glass of wine. Your Dad has a nice fire going in the fireplace."

"A fire?"

"I know, I know. How can a man who can no longer write his name build an absolutely perfect fire? I figure it's some primeval instinct that all men must possess. Fire-building, eating, and sex; they'll be the last to go."

"Too much information." Elizabeth waves her hands alongside her ears as if to deflect news that her father and I might be still somewhat normal. Too little or too much, that's always been a problem for Elizabeth.

Kevin is keeping a close watch on his fire, but he stands and opens his arms when he sees his daughter.

"Hey, Daddy," she says, "you're looking good." For once she sounds like herself, and for a short while we could be mistaken for a television family, most likely one from a Lifetime drama. Kevin pokes at his fire, nod-ding sympathetically as Elizabeth relates the highs and lows of her week. I pass around pumpkin bread and smile graciously.

Eventually, of course, she runs out of things to say and they both turn to me. Elizabeth is counting on me to fill in the silence, but Kevin begins to pester so steadily, I cannot think straight. *See if she'll look after the house while we're gone, Brenda. Tell her we need a week or two away and nothing much can go wrong in so short a time.*

"Elizabeth, your father is anxious to take a trip and I wondered if you have any suggestions for us."

Geez, Brenda. I said tell, not ask. You're opening a whole can of worms now.

"A trip where?" Elizabeth nervously watches Kevin flip embers like flapjacks and send sparks shooting up the chimney.

See? What did I tell you? She'll want us to go on some Senior Citizen Mentally Challenged Physically Impaired bus trip, for godsakes.

Then quit acting like a pyromaniac. I touch his sleeve, and he puts down the poker, settles back into his chair, and manages to look serene. "Somewhere warm," I tell Elizabeth. "Anyplace he can get out and move. You know being inside all these days has been hard on him. On both of us."

Not Florida. Kevin's fingers begin to drum a discordant tune on the arm of his chair. *I refuse to go to Florida.*

Elizabeth gives me one of her stern, calculating looks, a look I'm certain has a direct link to Kevin's no nonsense gene. "I don't think it's a good idea, Mom. Maybe it would work if I could go with you? Once Brant and I've picked our own wedding location?"

Absolutely not. Kevin's foot taps against the hearth.

"You've got too much to do, honey." I watch Kevin over my reading glasses, willing him back into submission. "Your father is so strong, so vital, so cooperative right now." The old voodoo is back at work. "This would be an excellent time. We'll be fine, honestly."

Sometimes you have to ask for help. Sometimes you have to admit you have no clue what to do next and be willing to take on faith what others tell you to do. Women like me learned this lesson as soon as we gave birth; men like Kevin are still holding out, refusing to surrender any outward show of control. Which is why I am completely honest with Marie, Elizabeth's travel agent, and why Kevin is not totally ecstatic when I replace his tattered travel brochures with a pristine cruise line booklet. He holds it unopened, resting atop his palms like a sacrificial offering, for a long time.

"Well? Whaddya think?" I finally ask.

Given our circumstances, he finally answers. *I guess this is good.*

"It will be great." I fire up the old magic spell. "We can eat good food and lie in the sun and watch the world go by."

He doesn't look convinced.

"What were you hoping for?" I ask.

Something edgy and new. A singular place where we'd be totally on our own.

I don't remind him that we're already in *that* place.

It has been years since Kevin and I took a cruise, and I have to admit I'm overwhelmed by the grand scale of everything now: the sheer size of The Kingdom of the Sea herself, the number of guests and crew, and the many, many lounges and bars and places to eat. I worry Kevin will wander off and never be found again, although Marie has assured me otherwise. "First of all, you're in a limited space, Mrs. Gorman, and the security is terrific. They know when you leave and re-board the ship, when you enter your cabin. There are cameras in all the public areas. It would be very difficult to simply disappear. Much harder than wandering off from a beachside resort, I'd say."

Aha.

At the moment, at least, Kevin is calm and sticking to my side and looking every bit the model tourist. Elizabeth would be proud to witness his polite nods to effusive staff members and his smiles to the ship photographer, his ease in navigating the luncheon buffet and his patience during the lifeboat drill. Although his silence bothers me. Is the clamor of the ship too loud for me to hear? Or have I lost my sense of his voice?

When the ship sets sail, we stand on the highest deck and wave to the folks along shore like everybody else. Kevin, I notice, is looking down, rather than off in the distance, and I take his arm and steer him away from the railing. "I bet you're tired. Do you want to go to our cabin?"

He shakes his head and plops down in a deck chair where we can listen to the steel drum band and watch a conga line dance around the pool on deck below us. *Ole, ole!* They sing, raising their arms skyward. Despite the music and the dancing and the children splashing in the pool and the loud conversations all around, I fall sound asleep and awake in a panic.

Oh, dear God. Kevin.

But Kevin is right here, watching me. "Did you nap?" I ask, looking around. The crowds have dwindled to a few couples, dressed for dinner and strolling along the deck. Below us, the pool has emptied and the hot tub has filled with tanned, silver-haired women, old friends, judging by their easy laughter. I check my watch. "Shall we shower and dress for dinner and then go for a drink?"

We have cocktails in the Nautilus Lounge, where a bald, goateed pianist plays music from our parents' heyday: Gershwin and Carmicheal and

Irving Berlin. "Bon Voyage," I say, clinking my glass against Kevin's to the strains of "Goodnight, Irene." He takes a sip, holding the liquid behind his cheeks before swallowing. Sitting here on our rounded leather banquette, I imagine we look pretty damn good. Not old and feeble, not young and overly chatty, but reasonably appealing and naturally comfortable in our silence. People pass by and smile like they, too, get our vibe and find it acceptable. The server has no trouble taking drink orders from me rather than Kevin. No problem with me signing the charge to our cabin.

The same is true at our table for two in the dining room. Kevin appears attentive while our waiter makes his recommendations, but when I do the ordering for both of us, Sanjay respectfully defers to me. "Thank you, madam," he says, taking our menus and bowing away from the table.

Kevin's fine motor skills have not slipped away from him yet, and he loves to eat, so dinner is a good time. Even the slow pace of serving one course after another does little to disturb him. "What now?" I ask as we finish our crème brulees. "A bit of dancing? A walk on the deck? Or would you like to go to the musical show?"

No response. No telepathy tonight.

"See you tomorrow." Sanjay pulls out my chair for me. "Tomorrow is formal. Dress up." His lively manner is lost on Kevin, who is drifting away from the table.

My knees have grown stiff from too much sitting. "Tomorrow." I repeat before hobbling into Kevin's wake.

Bad knees or not, I have decided I will walk as long and as late as Kevin wants to walk, because once we are sealed into our cabin, I worry claustrophobia may overcome us. We cruise through the casino, but the jangle of slot machines and clatter of coins makes us jittery. We pass through lounges where the music ranges from jazz to karaoke and eventually find ourselves outside the disco, where music from the Sixties, our music, calls to us like Sirens. We step into the room where floor to ceiling windows curve around the back of the ship like the panes of a lighthouse. Here folks of all ages are gyrating through a medley of old dance songs: The Twist, The Locomotion, The Pony, The Mashed Potatoes. The dancers look both ridiculous and amazingly beautiful, and I could easily stay here and watch them all night, but Kevin takes my hand and tugs me out into the corridor. "Loud," he says when we reach the elevators. "Too loud."

On the deck below the disco, the ship seems to be standing still, but the wind beats at our clothes and whips our hair back from our faces. The water below us is so black it can only be seen in the rise and fall of its white-tipped crests. "Alone at last," I shout to Kevin, who once again is staring straight down.

In that moment of facing an endless dark sky and sea, I feel myself shrink. I grow small and insignificant and frightened, and I use my last bit of self-control to urge Kevin away from the edge and around the corner where the rock-climbing wall serves as a windbreak. Above us the music has softened and slowed. "Blue Moon," always the last song at our high school dances, falls down around us, and now, as then, I want to be held. "Let's dance," I say.

Kevin's arms wrap around me, his chin rests against my temple, and we move together in our old familiar rhythm. Who would have guessed that dancing, like riding a bike and raising a child and finishing each other's thoughts, one of those acts average people perform with no professional training, would be the last to leave us? So when Kevin lowers his mouth to my ear and clearly says, "fly," I'm not the least bit surprised.

The rock-climbing wall is open only a short time each day. At night, it is decidedly off limits. We slip past the chain, past the warning sign, and position ourselves out of view of the wraparound disco windows. I slide off my new expensive, bought-especially-for-the-cruise panties, shove them into Kevin's pocket, and go to work on his belt. If there are security cameras, as Marie has promised, I can't find them. I am more concerned about a rock bruising my kidney as I nestle my back against the wall and pull Kevin into me. The footing is tricky, but after a bit of scrambling, I step out of my shoes and onto a low rocky projection, and we are ready for business.

"Remember the Alamo," I say, and from somewhere I hear Kevin laughing.

I'm with you, baby, he says. *It doesn't matter what happens next.*

He's right, of course.

If we are swept overboard or thrown off the ship for indecent behavior, if Kevin fades like a flower and never says another word, it will all come down to this: he will never leave me. As we move towards eternity, Kevin will be in my head, telling me which lawn guy to hire or when to move money from one fund to another or that I look mighty fine for an old broad. His steady presence will urge me on, echoing the rush of my blood, my breath, my heart.

It will be, I promise myself, like flying.

About the Author

Sara Kay Rupnik is a native of Northwestern Pennsylvania and now spends her time in Coastal Georgia, West Cork, Ireland, and Bexley, Ohio. She holds a M.F.A. in Writing from Vermont College and is co-founder of Around the Block Writers Collaborative. Her fiction, nominated for a Pushcart Prize and short-listed for the 2010 Sean O'Faolain Short Story Prize, appears in literary journals in the U.S. and the U.K. She teaches creative writing for the Jekyll Island Arts Association.

Other Recent Titles from Mayapple Press:

Jeannine Hall Gailey, *The Robot Scientist's Daughter*, 2015
        Paper, 84pp, $15.95 plus s&h
        ISBN 978-936419-42-5
Jessica Goodfellow, *Mendeleev's Mandala*, 2015
        Paper, 106pp, $15.95 plus s&h
        ISBN 978-936419-49-4
Sarah Carson, *Buick City*, 2015
        Paper, 68pp, $14.95 plus s&h
        ISBN 978-936419-48-7
Carlo Matos, *The Secret Correspondence of Loon and Fiasco*, 2014
        Paper, 110pp, $16.95 plus s&h
        ISBN 978-1-936419-46-3
Chris Green, *Resumé*, 2014
        Paper, 72pp, $15.95 plus s&h
        ISBN 978-1-936419-44-9
Paul Nemser, Tales of the Tetragrammaton, 2014
        Paper, 34pp, $12.95 plus s&h
        ISBN 978-1-936419-43-2
Catherine Anderson, *Woman with a Gambling Mania*, 2014
        Paper, 72pp, $15.95 plus s&h
        ISBN 978-1-936419-41-8
Victoria Fish, *A Brief Moment of Weightlessness*, 2014
        Paper, 132pp, $16.95 plus s&h
        ISBN 978-1-936419-40-1
Susana H. Case, *4 Rms w Vu*, 2014
        Paper, 72pp, $15.95 plus s&h
        ISBN 978-1-936419-39-5
Elizabeth Genovise, *A Different Harbor*, 2014
        Paper, 76pp, $15.95 plus s&h
        ISBN 978-1-936419-38-8
Marjorie Stelmach, *Without Angels*, 2014
        Paper, 74pp, $15.95 plus s&h
        ISBN 978-1-936419-37-1
David Lunde, *The Grandson of Heinrich Schliemann & Other Truths and Fictions*, 2014
        Paper, 62pp, $14.95 plus s&h
        ISBN 978-1-936419-36-4

For a complete catalog of Mayapple Press publications, please visit our website at *www.mayapplepress.com*. Books can be ordered direct from our website with secure on-line payment using PayPal, or by mail (check or money order). Or order through your local bookseller.